The Dating Experiment

The Dating Experiment

Elodia Strain

SWEETWATER
BOOKS
An Imprint of Cedar Fort, Inc.
Springville, Utah

ISBN 13: 978-1-4621-1956-1

Published by Sweetwater, an imprint of Cedar Fort, Inc.
2373 W. 700 S., Springville, UT 84663
Distributed by Cedar Fort, Inc., www.cedarfort.com

Library of Congress Cataloging-in-Publication Data on file

Cover design by Priscilla Chaves
Cover design © 2017 by Cedar Fort, Inc.
Edited and typeset by Jessica Romrell and Erica Myers

Printed in the United States of America

10 9 8 7 6 5 4 3 2 1

Printed on acid-free paper

To my dad, Mark Saavedra.
Thank you for showing me by example how to turn pain into compassion, sorrow into faith, and everything else into laughter.

Also by Elodia Strain

My Girlfriend's Boyfriend

Previously Engaged

The Icing on the Cake

# Chapter One

Here's the thing you need to know about me before I tell you everything else: I've never been very lucky. I am not the girl who things work out for. I'm the girl whose Schwinn gets sideswiped by the SUV being driven by the girl who things work out for.

So it shouldn't be much of a surprise that I'm sitting here, wearing a garage sale button-down that's about two and a half sizes too small, answering calls and trying not to get fired from my temp job at—*Brrriiing, Brrriiing*—Well, you're about to find out.

"Thank you for calling Totally True Tellings. This is Mystical Misty." I hit the spacebar on the computer, sending the tinkling wind chime sound into the phone. "How can I look into the future for you?"

The person on the other end was silent for a beat. "Um. I'm sorry. I've never called one of these things before. I'm not sure what I'm supposed to say."

"Do you have a question?" I asked in my most soothing tone. "A reason you called?"

"Kind of." The female voice on the line sounded young and a little sniffly. "It's about my boyfriend."

"Last chance to impress me." My boss Capri, who'd been listening in on my calls at random times all week, was loud in the left ear of my headset. The temp agency had placed me at True Tellings for six weeks while one of their perma psychics was out on maternity leave. But the way things were going, I might not make it to six *days*.

All because of few little reviews Capri found on Psychie—which is apparently the Yelp of the telephone psychic world.

Jetty W.
Misty had a nice pleasant voice, but when I asked her for some tips on good lotto numbers, she said, "Lotto numbers? Do you know all the things you have a better chance at than winning the lottery? Getting struck by lightning. Dying in a plane crash. Being wrongfully convicted of a crime." Obviously, I will not be calling again.

Mike D.
I like True Tellings a lot, but if you get Misty, HANG UP. When I asked her how I would know if I was in love with my girlfriend she said, "What is love? Baby don't hurt me. Don't hurt me. No more." The reading was free, but I still feel like I got ripped off.

Anonymous
Is there someone you hate? Someone you wish bad things would happen to? Then have them call this network and ask

*for Misty. If you yourself want a solid psychic reading, ask
for Fiona.*

That last one isn't really fair. Fiona has this really cool
British accent, so everything she tells people sounds good,
even if it's the exact same terrible advice I'm shelling out.

As for the other reviews, Capri made my profile on the
True Tellings website before meeting me.

So there I was, Photoshopped onto a tree swing, my
strawberry blonde waves way shinier than they've ever
been in real life, my green eyes kind of sparkling, with
this little blurb under my bare feet: Hello, friend. My
name is Misty. I love people and enjoy helping them find
their path in life. I have a special gift for guidance in the
areas of work, love, and wealth.

Problem is, Capri never asked me if I actually have a
special gift in those areas, and I really, really don't.

Here's a little glimpse into those areas of my own life
as proof.

Work: I was trained by the best in the Cal Teach pro-
gram at UC Berkeley and landed my dream job teaching
eighth grade science at Seattle's beloved Dalton Academy.
But I lost said dream job a mere month after school started
when I departed slightly from the curriculum, put on a
mad-scientist costume, and accidentally taught the kids
how to make toilet wine. Now I'm currently taking whatever jobs I can from the Aim High Temp Agency. Some
of the craziest I've had so far: beauty salon hair sweeper,
llama babysitter, and golf course water feature diver.

Love: I've only had two serious boyfriends my whole
life. One was a drummer I met my freshman year of college. He broke up with me when I told him I thought

Pete Best was the guy who invented mayonnaise. The other was Dillon, the cute, quiet pediatrician I met at a barbeque last fourth of July. Currently, he's about two months into a three-month Med Abroad trip that he said would be a good opportunity for him to "figure things out." The second such trip he's taken since we got together.

And then there's wealth: long story short, I've got none. I had to back out of a contract on a cute, cozy bungalow in Kirkland when I lost my job. Now I live with two roommates—my best friend from Berkeley and her Microsoft wunderkind cousin—in a downtown Seattle apartment four blocks from the fire station. And after selling my furniture, my wardrobe, and nearly half of the vinyl collection my dad helped me build, I'm still so broke I rubbed a lemon wedge under my arms for deodorant this morning.

All of that notwithstanding, Capri wanted me to dole out career, relationship, and wealth advice. So I was soldiering on. Trying to be the best darn telephone psychic I could be.

"All right. Your boyfriend is . . ." I closed my eyes like the *How to Be More Intuitive* book I'd found at the library suggested.

"He's going to break up with me, isn't he?"

"I'm not sure." My eyes were still closed. "But I'm seeing something round. Does that mean anything to you?"

"Something round?"

"Yes . . . like . . . roundishly round."

"Roundishly round?" Capri repeated softly.

"Is it . . . a basketball?" the girl ventured.

"Does he like basketball?" I asked.

"Yes."

"That might be it, then."

"Might be?" the girl said.

"Very possibly could be," I said.

"I know what it is," the caller sounded suddenly confident. "He doesn't think I support his dream of being in the NBA."

"Oh. And why do you think he thinks that?"

"I just told him a five foot seven guy who hasn't played basketball since fifth grade probably should look for another dream. He didn't like that very much."

"I see it," I said, Dillon shooting to the front of my mind. "It feels like he's a million miles away even though he's sitting right next to you?"

"Yes," the girl said emphatically.

"And he stopped texting you as often."

"Totally."

"And then, one day, he didn't save the last egg roll for you."

"What?"

"Oh." My eyes snapped open. "I just mean, you know, symbolically. He stopped saving the symbolic egg roll for you."

"Huh?"

"I really think the best thing to do is talk to him about it."

Bing bong. Your free one-minute reading is over. If you wish to continue please press or say "1" and have your credit card ready.

"Let me get my credit card!" the girl said.

"For real?"

"I guess your pathetic love life is a plus for me," Capri said into my ear. "Try to keep her on for at least five minutes."

And with a click she was gone.

I listen to True Tellings's disclaimer as I waited for the caller to enter the requisite info.

Please be advised, the reading you are about to receive is for entertainment purposes only and should not be considered as advice from a doctor, a psychologist, a life coach, a veterinarian, or any person trained, educated, or qualified in any field or subject whatsoever. If you choose to follow advice given, you do so at your own risk.

As the voice went on, I squeezed the foam University of Louisville baseball I kept in my cubicle. Ian, my high school best friend, had given it to me when he went there to pitch and became a really big deal in college baseball. Which led to him being a *really big* deal in professional baseball. I'm talking millions of followers on Instagram, been in *People* magazine, big. I'd squished the ball so much over the past ten years you could barely make out the cardinal's beak anymore.

"So how much is this?" My caller was back on the line.

"It's $4.99 a minute."

"Whoa. That's a little much. This is a prepaid credit card, and I think it only has, like, maybe four bucks left on it."

I knew what that was like. This past month, I've only had a positive bank balance twice. And once was due to a bank error. "Maybe you can call back some other time?"

"But we're right in the middle of this. Can't you just extend my time a little?"

"I really can't." The phone would click off in thirty seconds if she didn't input her credit card information. "I'm sorry." I kind of wanted to tell her she would have just as much—no, probably more—luck asking one of her closest friends about this stuff. But Capri might be back to listening in. And I really needed this job.

"So I just have to sit around and wonder if he's going to break up with me?"

"Um . . ." I looked around the call center, which was really just the basement of Capri's house near Seattle's famed Green Lake. The three other employees who were on the clock—Ling, Grady, and Fiona—were all occupied with various types of readings. "Maybe . . ."

I watched as the call clock on my computer counted down. Fifteen seconds. Fourteen seconds. Thirteen seconds.

I heard Capri talking on her cell upstairs and then the sound of the garage door opening.

"Get a pen," I whispered into the phone.

"What?"

"A pen. I'm going to give you my cell phone number. Then you can call me for free."

"Oh my gosh! That's so sweet of you!" She quickly took down my number. "I'll call you in a bit. You are the best! Thanks for ev—"

The phone hung up on her.

"Well. She'll call if she needs to." I whispered to no one. Then I adjusted my headset and rubbed my temples.

"How much longer 'til you get sprung?" asked Ling, a cute girl who works at True Tellings to support her career as a musician, now that she was finished with her call.

I pushed the power button on my phone. "Twenty-three minutes."

Ling twisted her inky black hair into a bun atop her head and secured it with a binder clip. "I thought of another one," she said, unsuccessfully fighting a yawn that made her eyes water. "An online class that teaches people how to teach online classes."

"Love it!" I said with a laugh.

In between calls, Ling and I like to come up with ideas for businesses we are going to start so *we* can watch Bravo TV in our pajamas all day and boss around the people who work for *us*.

"I thought of one too." I looked at my screen as it lit up. "Oh wait. I'm ringing."

I hit the A (answer call) key on my keyboard and saw that the caller had prepaid for ten minutes. I like prepaid calls, because I don't have to feel like a slimy salesperson to get minutes.

"Thank you for calling Totally True Tellings. This is Mystical Misty. How can I look into the future for you today?"

"Hello, Misty. My name is Viv. My usual psychic is on vacation with no cell service. But I'm sitting here trying to make a huge decision and I really need some guidance."

"That's what I'm here for." I hit the W key on my keyboard to cue the sound of gentle wind.

"Perfect," Viv said. "So. I'm just going to come out and ask: who should I hire for this teaching job?"

Teaching job? My ears perked up like a dog hearing the word *walk*.

"Hmm," I said as calmly as I could muster. "Maybe you could tell me a little bit about the job?"

"I'm the principal at Atlas Academy in Bellevue. And we really need a new science teacher."

Hang on a second.

A science teaching job at Atlas Academy.

Why did that sound so familiar?

And that's when I realized: I'd interviewed for that job. With a woman named Vivienne!

My heart slammed into my ribs as I realized I was talking to my interviewer.

"Well," I said, trying to keep my voice calm. "I think I can help you with that."

I squished the heck out of the cardinal. Obviously I couldn't come out and say, *Choose Gabby Malone or your life will be cursed forever.* But maybe I *could* use the time as a sort of bonus interview.

"I'm actually having strong feelings about this," I said quickly. "So I'm just going to jump in and say things if that's alright. Feel free to interrupt me whenever you like."

"Sounds great."

"Okay. I'm seeing a large number of applicants. Does that sound right?"

She let out a whistle. "We had over 400. We interviewed ten."

Wow. Over 400 applicants. It made sense. Atlas had an amazing reputation and everyone wanted to teach there. It was this cool, progressive school with trendy street-art painted buildings, an organic school garden, and a course catalog that included everything from Algebra to Urban Chicken Cooping. And it paid well. Really well.

"I'm seeing an interview with a young woman with an ee sound at the end of her name," I said. "Like Abby? Kathy? Maddy?"

I waited for Viv to say, "Yes! It's Gabby! She was clearly the best. Some might say she had an unorthodox interview, but I feel like I really understood her."

But nothing.

"Ashley? Nancy?" I tried again.

"Odette." Vivienne sighed. "That's who I'm leaning toward. I think."

Odette Frank. I knew exactly who she was. She student taught at Dalton and by all accounts was this super cool teacher girl. She spoke three languages and had taught school in Paris. She drove a 1967 Corvette. She rocked heels one minute and kicked them off to play a game of soccer the next.

I, on the other hand, am not a super cool teacher girl. Some proof? I answered Vivienne's interview question, "What does Gabby Malone do for fun on Friday nights?" with, "Sometimes I drive out to Cle Elum and quilt with my Aunt's quilt group. . . . I'm pretty good at knitting, and I've gotten really into couponing lately."

I narrowed my eyes, remembering seeing Odette at Atlas that day.

"Odette . . ." I said to Vivienne. "I'm seeing different countries. Maybe different languages. Does that mean anything to you?"

"Whoa." Vivienne sounded shocked. "That definitely means something."

Man. If only I always knew who and what I was talking about, I could be an awesome psychic.

I quickly racked my brain for any inside scoop on Odette.

"But wait." I gave a tiny gasp. "I see something in her past."

"What do you mean?"

"I mean . . ." Suddenly a memory struck. "I see a road trip from Washington to California in a rental car that wasn't supposed to leave the state." I paused dramatically. "And a swimsuit she returned. After wearing it."

"Wow," Vivienne said.

"Yeah." I said with a sigh. "Sorry about that."

"Sorry? About what? The more I find out about the woman the more I see she has really *lived*. That she can understand what is facing teens today. She's just what we need. You know, it's true what they say about just trusting your gut."

What the what?

"Thank you so much, Misty," Viv said.

"Wait!" I shouted so loudly I made poor Grady jump. "You have three minutes left. And more is coming through."

"Really?"

"Yes! Really. I'm seeing another candidate. A mid-twenties woman with light hair and a vintage polka dot dress. I'm seeing her telling you a joke."

"Oh. The woman who said, 'Did you hear oxygen went on a date with potassium? It went OK.'"

"Yes!" I squeaked, feeling embarrassed all over at my terrible small talk skills. I always say way too much or way too little. Too little: "So . . . today . . . there's weather." Too much: "So . . . today . . . I'm having a lot of post-nasal drip." This time, I'd gone with a joke.

"I think that candidate is out of the running," Vivienne continued. "She was kind of a mess."

"Yes, but so are teens today! Right? They are epic messes! What with too much tech and GMO food and Zayn leaving One Direction."

"Interesting . . . I think I see where you're going here."

"I think perhaps the universe wants you to make sure you didn't overlook people who made little mistakes. In fact, I see a girl who made a few. Maybe she hummed *Eye of the Tiger* while she waited outside your office to get herself pumped up and didn't realize you could hear it. Maybe she grabbed five of the lollipops off your desk when she thought you weren't looking. And maybe she denied taking them when you asked. Maybe she said her favorite inspirational quote was, *It's on like Donkey Kong.*"

"Wow," Vivienne said. "That was all . . . oddly specific. And right on the nose. I think I might dump my regular psychic. What's your name again? So I can get you directly next time?"

Next time? I couldn't do this again.

Bing bong. Would you like to add minutes to your reading?

"Hello? Are you still there?" Vivienne's voice came into my ear.

"I'm here," I said. "Maybe you should just add more minutes to this reading. I feel like I'm really on right now, you know?"

"Yes, well, you've been great, but I have so much to do! Thank you!" And with that, she hung up.

And I just knew: Odette Frank was getting the job.

I exhaled and moved to tear off my headset.

But before I could, another call came in. I glanced at my computer: another prepaid reading. This one for five minutes. Nice.

"Thank you for calling Totally True Tellings where our Tellings are Truly True," I said, going with another of our approved greetings. "This is Mystical Misty. How can I look into the future for you?"

"Well," a raspy young voice said, "Mystical Misty, you can tell me if I'm going to be let out of this place in time to go with Kent Ralston to the Homecoming dance."

"Okay," I said. "I can try that."

"Cool. Because I don't know how much longer I can stand it in here. They said it could be up to three months this time."

"Uh huh." I gulped.

"Last time, I was locked up for almost a month, and I legit almost lost my mind."

"Um." I lowered my voice. "You're not, like, calling from prison are you?"

She laughed. "No. Though it's not much of a step up. I'm holed up in the hospital."

"Oh." I blinked. "I'm sorry."

"So is my college fund," the girl joked.

I was both a bit shocked and a bit touched by her pluck.

"Yep. I've been in and out of good ole' Seattle Pediatric since I was born. All seventeen years."

"Seattle Pediatric," I repeated. "I have a friend who's a nurse there."

"Yeah. Nurse Paige. She let me use her credit card number for this call. She said I could have five minutes."

Whoa. That was twenty-five bucks. And so the kind of thing Paige would do.

"I hope you don't mind me asking—"

"What's wrong with me?" she said before I could finish. "Congenital heart defect. Basically I come in here way too much and they try to keep me from kicking the bucket."

I didn't know how to respond.

"So, Misty—which, come on, is so not your real name—am I going to get out of here?"

There was a tiny crack in her voice that betrayed the pain and fear she was obviously feeling.

"It's Gabby," I confided, taking a second to look around first. "And this is a rare moment when I wish I were an amazing, truly gifted psychic with foresight."

"I would have been freaked out if you said anything else," the girl said. "Now I feel good leaving you a killer review."

"A good review!" I practically yelled.

"It's my GLA of the day."

"GLA?" I repeated. "As in, Gamma Lineolic Acid?"

"Um, no." She paused. I'm sure to roll her eyes. "It stands for Good Little Anything. It's for my blog: Project Good Little Anything."

"Project Good Little Anything." I opened up a web browser and quickly found the site.

"Wow." I sized up the photo at the top of the page. A girl with stunning blue eyes and blonde hair with blue tips, flashing a peace sign with one hand and holding a hardcover book in the other. "You're beautiful."

"Thanks," she said softly.

My eyes moved swiftly over the words on the page. "Do you mind if I read this really quick?"

"Go ahead," she said. "I'll blame you if Nurse Paige asks."

Welcome to Project Good Little Anything!
About Me: I'm Lennox. Reader. Writer. Glitter nail polish
addict. Sour candy devourer. Seattle Pediatric Hospital fre-
quent flyer.

"I'm so with you on the sour candy," I said.
"Right?" she responded.
Then I got back to reading.

About Project GLA: It started out as a beat up black note-
book with a Radiohead sticker on the front. It was a miser-
able day. I wanted to punch the phlebotomist. Stab my hos-
pital bed. Scream that I couldn't do anything. And then I got
this pic from my best friend, Kenley. She was at the football
game holding up a box of Lemonheads, and she'd captioned
it, "Thinking of you!!"
And it hit me like the punch I wanted to deliver to that
phlebotomist's face: For Kenley, it was just a text. Five sec-
onds, maybe. But for me, in that moment, it was every-
thing. Because it was pure goodness. That's when I decided I
would write down at least one good thing I did (or saw) in
a day. No matter how small. Seriously, sometimes all I could
do was smile at my favorite nurse. But it was something. A
Good Little Anything.
About the Blog: Soon I took my notebook online and
invited anyone who wanted to join the project. Practically
overnight, I was getting photos, videos, written accounts of
your own GLAs and the hashtags #goodlittleanything, #pro-
jectGLA, and many more were born. Soon came #thanksfo-
ranything from the people who wanted to make note of the
things other people did for them.

"This is so . . . incredible," I said into the phone as I read.

Bing bong.

"Oh no! That's the thirty second warning! I ate up all the time reading your blog." I wiped my tearing eyes with the cuff of my button down.

"No problem," Lennox said.

"I have to give you something. I know! How about your horoscope?"

"Sounds cool."

"All right. Let's start with your sign."

"I'm a—"

"Don't say it!" I held up my hand totally unnecessarily. I really, really wanted to give this girl a heck of a reading. "I'm feeling that you're an . . . aer . . . vir . . . can . . ."

"I'm a Leo," she said.

"Ah yes!" I said. "The sign of the mighty lion."

I think.

"Okay, Leo. Let's see." I thought back on the horoscopes I've read. Then I just said how I felt in horoscope language. "You are wise beyond your years and have the ability to make great things happen. Others are drawn to you and uplifted by you."

"Thanks, Gabby," Lennox said.

"Oh yeah!" I quickly added. "And Mercury is in retrograde, um, sometime, so, you know, watch out for that."

"Thanks." I could hear a soft laugh in her voice. "And, hey, maybe I'll call back sometime."

"I would love that," I said. "You can find my number in Paige's phone."

"Maybe I will."

"Thanks for calling, Lennox."

And then the phone clicked off.

I spent the next hour fielding quick calls and bingeing on Lennox's blog.

I was reading a list of GLAs made by a fourth-grade class—*my sister punched me and I didn't punch back, I painted my mom's nails, I gave my teacher a flower*—when I jumped at the sound of my Paige's voice behind me.

"Is that Lennox's blog?"

"Yes!" I tore off my headset. "This girl is amazing."

"Agreed," Paige said. "I miss the babies in the NICU, but being in Peds has its magic too."

I grabbed my blue chevron-patterned umbrella from beneath my desk. I'm pretty much the only Seattleite who carries an umbrella. But I didn't grow up here, so I guess that's my excuse. "Thanks for picking me up, by the way."

Blue Bertha, my 1999 Toyota Corolla, was completely out of gas.

"Of course." Paige put an arm around me. "It's only a couple miles out of the way. Hi, Ling." Paige waved her thin fingers in the air. "How's your grandma?"

"Good." Ling made a grateful expression. "She's able to walk with a walker now."

The fact that she remembers and legitimately cares about people is just one of the things I love about Paige.

"Do I hear an angel in here?" Grady, the University of Washington student and resident pet psychic who, like every guy on earth, fell in love with Paige the second he saw her, did his best cool guy strut into the room. "Paige," he said, absently adjusting his hat as he eyed her long legs in skinny jeans and booties, grey top, and three perfectly layered necklaces. "Do you have any raisins?"

"No raisins. But I might have a granola bar." Paige rooted through her Feed tote, which is covered in various pins and patches from her travels, causes, etc.

"Sorry, Grady, no granola bar."

Grady grabbed a chair and sat down in it backwards. "Well then, how about a date?"

"Oh sweetie." Paige's lips and eyes both turned up to the ceiling. "You're not even old enough to rent a car. Plus, I don't think my boyfriend would like that very much."

The full truth was that Paige didn't actually have a boyfriend. But she had a TON of exes who had no problem if she used them to get out of things—or get in to things—because they were all still madly in love with her.

Grady pulled his fist to his heart as if he'd been injured. "And again, she rejects me."

Paige winked at him then threw open the door and we headed up the concrete steps into the chilly fall evening.

Paige Sanchez is the absolute best. We met during freshman orientation at Berkeley, where I learned that she was from Bellevue, Washington, and she learned I was from whatever KOA campground my vagabond parents decided to park our camper at. After graduation, she backpacked through Europe and dabbled in making her own jewelry. Then, right around the time I was finished with my four-year stint at a small charter school in Oregon, she got a great job as a nurse at Seattle Pediatric and helped me land my job at Dalton. She's about a hundred times cooler than I am. Her Jeep almost always has a kayak or a paddleboard or a mountain bike strapped to it, waiting for her next big adventure. She has a bucket list that's full of things I would be terrified of. She can eat an endless amount of Oreos, knows how to do a killer cat eye, and has really been here for me over the past month.

"Here." As we crossed the grass yard, Paige reached into her bag and handed me a stack of fliers.

I instantly knew what they were: research studies.

Paige teaches an evening course at Pacific Credence University on Mondays and picks them up for me from the campus bulletin boards. And she sometimes tears down the best ones so no one else will apply.

I flipped through the stack as I climbed into Paige's mud-covered Jeep.

Let's see what we have here . . .

Nail Biting and Germs Study.

Reptile Adoption Study.

How Do You Study Study.

"Check this one out." At a stop sign, Paige reached over and plucked a bright pink flier from the back of the stack. "It looks pretty promising."

I focused on the small print on the page, which was kind of hard given that I was going on day sixty-something of my one-day contacts.

Researchers at Pacific Credence University, in partnership with Cupidity Dating app developers, are seeking single women between the ages of 21 and 35 to participate in a six-week study examining the role of social media mobile dating applications in modern dating.

The study requires a one-hour per week commitment over the course of six weeks and will include a relationship assessment, a speed dating session, and a conclusion seminar.

There are no major risks associated with this study. All applicants will be compensated with $300 per study week, and meals and travel expenses will be covered up to $200.

"$500 a week," I said. "This can't be for real."

"Already checked," Paige said. "It is."

"$500 a week."

I gazed out the window, visions of being a little less broke dancing in my head. I could eat brand name peanut butter again. I could buy a new pillow instead of using the stuffing from all my old stuffed animals. I could shave my legs without fear that I'd need a tetanus booster—which I couldn't afford—if I got a nick.

I refocused on the flier.

To find out if you qualify, please visit www.thedatingexperiment.web.

Cindy Chan, PhD & Brooke A. Whitmore, PhD, Lead Researchers

"I can't be in a dating experiment." I shuffled the flier to the bottom of the stack. "I might have a boyfriend. And he might be coming back in less than a month. And we might end up living happily ever after."

Paige opened her mouth. Then closed it. Then opened it again. And closed it again.

"Say it," I sighed. "You know you will eventually."

"I just think it's crazy that you're just sitting around while Dillon is in Mexico doing who knows what with Daphne the dermatologist."

Paige had been with me when I googled Dr. Daphne Douglas, after Dillon mentioned she was going on the trip to Mexico. She was gorgeous. Which really wasn't fair to her patients. They go to see her feeling all awful about their cystic acne, and she gives them a cream and a sympathetic smile on her perfect face.

"Thanks for the reminder," I said flatly.

"I just mean . . . you should be out there, living life, having fun. Dance outside in a lightning storm. Kiss three guys in one night. Run through the sprinklers on the courthouse lawn."

"Those are things *you* could get away with doing," I said. "But not me. And you wanna know why? Because I'd get struck. I'd get mono. And I'd get arrested."

"Well at least that would be an adventure." Paige flicked on her blinker. "You've got to live more, Gabby." She looked over at me. "Just say you'll think about the study."

"I'll think about it," I promised.

"Awesome." She cranked up the stereo. "Next I'll convince you to get a tattoo."

"I don't think so." I rested my head against the headrest and closed my eyes, enjoying the feeling of fresh air hitting my face through my open window as we drove.

My phone rang as Paige was pulling into the resident parking lot of our apartment complex.

Unknown Number.

I flung the heavy door open and shook my head as if to wake up my brain. "Well." I looked over the top of the car at Paige. "What should I tell a girl who wants to know if her boyfriend is about to break up with her?"

"Tell her that you know about an awesome dating study if he does."

"Hello?" I walked toward the lobby and Paige kept pace with me. "This is Misty."

"Gabby?" The voice on the line said.

I stopped dead in my tracks and a man in a red car swerved to miss hitting me.

Because it was not the girl with boyfriend problems on the phone. It was . . . "Dillon?"

Paige narrowed her eyes.

"Hello, beautiful." Dillon's voice washed over me like a warm, bubbly bath.

"Oh my goodness." I felt like I was melting from the inside out. "It's so good to hear your voice."

"Good to know." Dillon laughed into the phone. Oh my gosh I missed his laugh. "How would you feel about hearing it live pretty soon?"

"What do you mean *live*?"

"I'm at the airport in Guadalajara," Dillon said. "I'm coming home early. Tonight, actually. The past couple days I've been thinking a lot. And the thing is . . . I just really need to see you."

"You're coming home because you really need to see me?"

"Pretty much," Dillon answered.

I could just make out a string of announcements being made in Spanish.

"Sorry, Gab." I heard a rustling sound on the phone. "I have to go. But. Man. I'm just going to ask . . . can we meet tonight?"

"Yes." My mind raced in a million different directions. "Of course."

"What time is too late?"

"Anytime is fine," I answered before he even finished asking the question.

"I'll call you the second I land," Dillon promised. "I think my flight comes in just before midnight."

"Fly safe."

"I'll see you as soon as humanly possible."

"Okay."

"Bye, Gab." And then he was gone.

I pulled the phone away from my ear and stared at it.

"He's coming back?" Paige's voice jarred me into reality.

I nodded.

"When?"

"Tonight." I was still staring at the phone.

"I guess I'll hold onto this." Paige grabbed the pink flier and shoved it back in her bag.

Chapter Two

Ten minutes.

In ten minutes, Dillon Maxwell was meeting me at the cute little café where we had our first date.

I absently cradled a mug of chamomile tea as I thought back to that rainy Saturday afternoon last year.

It was the first weekend in August a few weeks after we first met. I was in my favorite blue Hunter boots and a floral cotton dress. I even paid a lot of money for a blowout at a fancy blow dry bar. (That was back when I had money to spend on those kinds of things. Now, I have a pedicure that I traded my roommate Iris four hours of face massages for.) When I spotted Dillon sitting at a table in the corner, doing the word jumble in the *Seattle Times*, I shook off my yellow umbrella and carried it at my side.

Dillon looked brainy-cute in a button down, jeans, and black-framed glasses. His dark hair was neatly cut with the tiniest bit of a cowlick, and his square jaw was cleanly shaven. He stood when I got to the table and pulled my chair out for me. And then, when I asked him about the black-marker mustache he had on his pointer finger, he held it up to his face and told me a corny joke he used when talking to a scared kid who had to get stitches.

And at that moment, I knew I was going to be a total goner.

The next five months were a blur of wonderfulness.

We went out on Tuesdays and stayed in on Fridays. He read thick books as I graded papers, my feet resting in his lap. We watched his favorite black and white movies and ate frozen pizza with homemade salad. I tracked down a vintage stethoscope for his birthday, and he said it was the best gift he'd ever received. He took me to his parents place near Portland for Thanksgiving. We helped Aunt Kit decorate the B&B for Christmas. We rang in the New Year at the Pacific Science Center.

It was perfect. And serious. Which, it turns out, freaked Dillon out.

I kind of started to get the hint when he gave me a 1,000-piece puzzle of Mount Rushmore for Valentine's Day. A place I've neither been nor talked about wanting to visit.

So we had The Talk. He said he thought we should take a break. I was heartbroken, but at the same time, almost grateful. Because I knew if things had continued in all their blissful wonder, I would have been completely shattered if/when it ended.

Then, to my surprise, Dillon called at the end of February and told me he missed me. After many long talks, we got back together, and this time I was all in. Because this was obviously it—capital I, capital T.

But, alas, you know how well that worked out for me. Dillon left me for Mexico, and I spent the past month having a recurring nightmare of Dr. Daphne coyly whispering words like "epidermis" and "rosacea" into his ear and him not being able to resist her.

My phone dinged and my heart burned in my chest.

My hands shook as I turned it over.

But it wasn't Dillon.

It was Paige.

Remember my advice.

Paige had given me a few tips to follow when I practically started hyperventilating at the thought of seeing Dillon.

"He was supposed to be there for three months!" I said. "The last time I saw him I had a job and an offer on a house, and I was using soap that didn't smell like a weird man."

"This is actually perfect," Paige had said. "You get too into your head when you plan things. Now you can just be . . . chill."

Just be chill.

Oh yeah.

That was easy for Paige to say. Paige is the epitome of chill. She is the queen of road tripping. She changed her major TWO times. She looks gorgeous in jeans, a rock band tee, and a swipe of cherry ChapStick.

I am the antithesis of chill. Especially when it concerns dating or anything dating adjacent. I show up to dates in tutus and glitter flats when I should be wearing cut offs and hiking boots. I talk about why bile tastes so terrible when I should talk about, well, anything else. I even once saw a fellow teacher I had a crush on at the drugstore, and when I looked at the stuff in his cart, I said, "Oh you're a Charmin Ultra Soft guy. Good to know."

I mean, seriously? Good to know? What the heck for?

Still, I consulted the How to Be Chill note Paige had typed into my phone. (After she dressed me in a black sweater, grey jeans, and slouchy knit cap.)

When he gets there, have earbuds in your ears.

I put my headphones in my ears and selected the Hipster BBQ station on Pandora. Whatever the heck a hipster BBQ is.

All right. I can do this. I can be cool.

I bobbed my head to the music and started snapping my fingers at my side. I caught my reflection in the window. I looked like the Fonz.

So I sat on my hands.

And that's when the café door opened. And he walked in.

And suddenly I realized: Paige was totally and completely right. I needed to play it cool.

Because if I didn't, I was in trouble.

Very. Big. Trouble.

Dillon just looked so . . . good. Like, not fair good. His chin was covered in the stubble I secretly love. His hair was longer and lighter at the tips. He was tan and dressed in jeans and a Med Abroad tee that made him look all do-good-y and perfect.

"Gabby!" He practically jogged toward me and my insides burned at the sight of him.

"Dillon!" My voice was crazy high. I hopped up and the headphones pulled me down. I quickly pulled them from my ears. "How the heck are you?"

Dillon leaned in for a hug, and I jumped back and did a weird mime move before giving him an exaggerated fist bump. "Pound it out Dill . . . pickle."

"What?" He bumped his fist into mine. And that tiny touch sent an electric-like current through me.

Not. Good.

"You must be wiped." I said, pointing to the chair across from mine. "Grab some wood."

Dillon plunked down in the chair across from mine and just kind of looked at me.

"You hungry for anything?" I asked him.

"I can't even tell anymore." Dillon kept his eyes on me. "You look good, Gabby. Really, really good. What have you been up to that has you looking this good?"

Why did he have to keep saying *good* like that?

"Oh, I've been up to a lot," I answered. "Cool stuff mostly."

"Like?"

"You know. Chilling, mostly. Chilling out, maxing, relaxing all cool and all."

Dillon's mouth twitched. "Isn't that from . . . *The Fresh Prince of Bel-Air*?"

Oh my gosh, it totally was. "I don't believe so."

I know my face turned instantly red. That's the thing about being a fair-skinned blonde. I blush. I splotch. Luckily, tonight Paige had lent me her major concealer.

"Interesting." Dillon narrowed his eyes like I was a mystery he was trying to solve.

"Anyway," I continued. "In addition to all the chilling, I've been doing a lot of other cool stuff. I've been staying up past eleven, like, every night."

"I missed you, Gab." Dillon reached for my hands, which were resting on the table.

And there it went. All my cool. "You did?"

"You opened up my world. Beat me at badminton. Got me addicted to key lime sherbet." Dillon gazed out the window. "I'll always love you for that."

And that's when the blood drained from my face. Because I knew. Just by the sound of his voice. That everything was about to come crashing down.

"But?" I said, uttering the word for him.

"Why do you think there's a but?" Dillon asked.

Because I'm me. Unlucky Gabby. And you're you. Amazing Doctor Dillon.

"I just . . . know there's one."

Dillon cleared his throat about five times. "I met someone. In Mexico."

It was like someone had grabbed my insides and twisted them. "Daphne the dermatologist?" I choked out.

"What? No." He shifted in his seat. "I went to high school with her. Her name is Daisy and she—"

I held my eyes shut, as if doing so would stop my brain from flipping through his high school yearbook.

"Sorry." Dillon's voice softened. "You probably didn't need to hear—"

"Nope."

"I just thought I owed it to you to—"

"Yep."

"Gabby." His voice was soft, almost pitiful.

I forced my eyes open, and the tears burned my cheeks.

"I'm so sorry."

"Don't be." I wiped the tears with the back of my hand. "It's fine. Good, actually. Now I can continue on with my super cool life." It was lame. Possibly the single lamest thing being spoken in the whole world at that precise moment. But it was all I had.

If only I really could *totally tell* the future . . . then I never would have said hello to him at that barbeque. Never would have decided to give it everything when he asked me for another chance. Never would have agreed to meet him at our café in the middle of the night.

And most of all, I never would have thought that something like happily ever after could happen to me.

Chapter Three

"Gabby? Are you alive in there?" Paige's muffled voice sounded through my bedroom door.

I shifted my head on my pillow and opened my eyes about half an inch. The sun was streaming in through the blinds, but I wasn't sure what time it was. Heck, I wasn't entirely sure what *day* it was. Friday, I was pretty sure.

"There's no one named Gabby here," I said. "She died of heartbreak."

I turned up the Love Sucks playlist I'd made on Spotify.

"What are you doing home?" Paige asked. "Shouldn't you be at work?"

"Capri told me to take a couple days off," I said.

It happened after she listened in on one of my first post-heartbreak calls, which went like this:

"Thank you for calling whatever the heck it's called." My voice was morose and robotic. "This is Misty. What do you want?"

"Hello, Misty," a male voice said. "I'm calling for some love advice."

"Love advice?" I harrumphed. "Let me guess, you need help figuring out how to smash a girl's heart to pieces?"

"No . . ."

"Never mind that she's done everything she could to be a great girlfriend. Never mind that she pulled that bee stinger out of your foot, even though you're a doctor and perfectly capable of doing it yourself."

"I'm confused—"

"Oh please. You know exactly what I'm talking about."

And that's when Capri told me she should fire me, but she needed me, so I better go home and get it together.

Ever since then, I'd been hunkered down in my bedroom, living on salt and vinegar potato chips, watching any and every reality TV show with the word *Extreme* in the title, and busying myself with a Dillon cleanse.

First, I cut Dillon's head out of all of the pictures on my bulletin board and replaced them with known villians: Darth Vader, Joseph Stalin, Dan Scott from *One Tree Hill*.

Then, I got to work on the Terrible Things about Dillon Maxwell list my roommates had slipped under my door. So far I'd added a pathetic two things:

1. He eats his hamburgers with a fork
2. He blamed me one time when he forgot where he parked the car when we went to The Crab Pot for dinner

"How's the list?" Paige asked me, her head poking in through the now-ajar door.

"I've written tons of things," I lied as I grabbed a piece of paper from my nightstand and held it up.

Paige nodded to Iris, who appeared from nowhere and grabbed the paper before I could stop her. "This is a list of overdue library books. You owe . . . geez a $34 fine on a book called, *How to Make Better Financial Decisions.*"

"I'm a loser!" I covered my face with a pillow.

I used to think I was tough. I mean, I've been washing my hair with a dollar store brand that makes my scalp feel like it's going to fall off. I had kidney stones during the SAT and I still took it.

But this?

I was no match for this.

Paige made a beeline for the bed, her homemade salsa in one hand, chips in the other. "Oh our poor little Gabby." She plopped down beside me, set the cupcake on my nightstand, and rubbed the top of my head. With her free hand she grabbed the actual list. "We have some stuff to add to this. Iris: the pen."

Iris nodded and produced a ballpoint pen.

"If he ordered any type of French food, he always ordered it in French," Paige said. "Even at IHOP."

"Ugh." Iris pulled a face. "The worst. I'm just going to draw someone barfing for that one."

"Yeah." I chuckled to myself for the first time in what felt like forever. "That was pretty silly."

"Now write *socks*," Paige instructed. "He was always wearing fancy socks. Even with tennis shoes. Striped. Argyle. Paisley. Hello? Ever heard of black socks buddy?"

"I didn't hate his socks," I said miserably.

"Well then I hate you," Iris deadpanned, shooting me her patented surly look.

"I've got one," I said softly.

Paige clapped. "She's got one!"

"I kind of hate how he calls his buddies *bruh.* 'Hey, *bruh.* How's it going, *bruh?*' I mean, he told me what *tension pneumothorax* means when we were watching *Grey's Anatomy,* but he can't say *bro?* What the heck?"

"Add it! Add it!" Paige chanted. "See." She squeezed my shoulders in satisfaction. "We're making progress."

"And now." Iris handed me three laser-printed photos of some guys. They looked vaguely familiar.

But why . . .

"Oh my gosh!" I threw them onto the bed like hot potatoes. "Is that Dillon?"

"Age progression photos," Iris said flatly. "That's him at age 40, 50, and 60. I took into account the erratic hours he works, the fact that I've never once seen him use sunscreen, and his penchant for breaking hearts, which will eventually catch up to him. Looks like you dodged a bullet to me."

I tried to look at the photos again, but it was just too freaky seeing Dillon's face all weathered and wrinkly. Instead, I just sank further back into my pillow and sighed. "I guess so."

"Keep those for when you're feeling weak." Iris nodded her dark blue hair toward the photos.

"Thanks, Iris."

She didn't respond, just blinked at me. And I was immediately reminded of my first night in the apartment. I woke up thirsty at about two o'clock in the morning and found Iris sharpening the kitchen knives. "It relaxes me," she said unprompted before I stumbled back to bed, shoved a couple suitcases in front of my door, and slept with my phone in my hand.

"Seriously, guys." I felt a tiny smile form on my lips. "I appreciate all of this."

My phone dinged.

Paige quickly picked it up and read the text on the screen. "So," she said, holding the phone to her chest. "Don't be mad."

"Don't be mad about what?" I reached for the cell, my bloodshot eyes widening. "What did you do?"

She relinquished the phone and I read the message myself.

Thank you for your interest in The Impact of Social Media and Mobile Applications on the Outcome of Modern Relationships aka the Five Fridays Dating Experiment! We've sent you an email with a link to the online application. We sincerely hope you're a match for our study!

Cindy Chan, PhD & Brooke A. Whitmore, PhD, Lead Researchers

"When did I express interest in the Five Fridays Dating Experiment?" I asked.

"When I filled out the *I am Interested in this Study* form from your email account," Paige said, biting her lip.

"What?" I stared at her. "Do I look like a girl who wants to date? Dating did this." I threw off my blanket and pointed to my Berkeley sweats, my t-shirt covered in grease spots from my chip habit, and my swollen face.

"I love you, Gabs," Paige said. "A friend is supposed to do what she thinks is best for you."

She patted the top of my head.

"I've already started filling out the application for you."

"What?" I asked, shock taking over my face.

"The first part says to get a friend to help!" Paige explained. "It's just questions about you . . . and . . . your love life. But, most importantly, you get a $100 Visa gift card just for emailing it back."

"That can't be true," I said, narrowing my eyes with skepticism. "It's an application. If I send it in, that means I'm applying for the study."

"I don't think so." Paige ran out of the room and grabbed her laptop. Mine only works on Tuesdays. For real. Not even Iris—Microsoft IT superheroine herself—can figure it out. Paige dropped the computer in front of me and after a few moments of booting, etc., she pointed to the screen. "See? There at the bottom. It says, *Filling out this application does not mean you will be part of the study*. And look, it's like half done."

"So I guess we're done talking about how much we hate Dillon?" Iris asked.

"We're done for now," Paige said.

"Let me know if you get back to something interesting," Iris said as she disappeared down the hall. "Or if you need me to hack into any of his accounts."

I gave Paige a freaked-out look. She just shrugged.

Iris is a bit of a mystery. I know that she works for Microsoft during the week, she works at the Medieval Village on the weekends, and she knows way too much about things like fake passports, Krav Maga, and tasteless poisons.

Paige is convinced she's some sort of secret government agent.

I rested my back against my bed pillows and focused on the laptop.

Welcome to the Five Fridays Dating Study! In order for us to get to know you better, please fill out the questionnaire below. We promise, it will only take about ten minutes. And as a thank you, you will receive a $100 Visa gift card to use anywhere Visa is accepted!

Thanks,
Cindy Chan, PhD & Brooke A. Whitmore, PhD, Lead Researchers

$100 for ten minutes. That was $10 a minute. I barely made $10 an *hour* as a temp.

"All right." I crisscrossed my legs and positioned the computer in front of me on the bed. "So basically I fill this out to see if I qualify for the study?"

"Yes," Paige said as she squished up beside me.

"And since I'm fairly sure I won't qualify for the study, I'm just providing additional data for the study authors to use in their abstract."

"Sure," Paige said. "You weirdo."

"I guess I can do that for $100." I looked up at the ceiling to mimic dreaming. "Telling myself I'm having a Vanilla Bean shake from Hot Cakes while drinking watered-down powdered milk doesn't exactly work."

"All the more reason," Paige said, pointing to the computer.

I leaned forward and read what Paige had already filled out on the application.

About You: Five Questions
(For these questions, you get to have a friend help you!
How fun is that? Now . . . tell us everything!)

1. **In five words or less, how would your friends describe you?** Loyal. Hardworking. Creative. Romantic. Terrible Cook.

"That's six words," I said. "And you forgot heartbroken and miserable."

"Nope." Paige shook her head. "I'm the friend. I get to write what I think, thank you very much."

I took in a big breath. "Okay."

2. **What was the last movie you watched?** *Hope Floats.*

"That one was easy," Paige said.

"Except it's wrong," I said as I moved a hand over my mouth.

"I heard you re-watch the part where 'To Make You Feel My Love' is playing five times last night," Paige countered.

She was right. *Hope Floats* is my crying movie.

Paige gave me a hug. "I'm sorry, sweetie. Let's just keep chugging along."

3. **Name a few things your friends would say you're really good at:**

Paige hadn't gotten to that one, so I asked her, "What am I really good at?"

She named off a list without missing a beat. "Vintage clothes shopping. Putting others before yourself. Guessing how many anything (candies, pennies, gumballs) are in a jar. Taking a five-minute shower. And, since I know you'd want this to be completely accurate, hula-hooping."

I laughed, and it was like with each laugh, my body felt a little bit better.

4. Name a few things your friends would say you're not so good at:

"Here's your chance to say cooking," I said.

"Cooking," Paige said quickly. "Small talk. Fixing things. Taking compliments. And . . . whistling. If only you could whistle *and* hula-hoop," Paige said. "Then you'd be unstoppable." Paige speed-read through the next questions. "Looks like the rest is on you," she said, and I rested my head on her shoulder. "Thank you, Paige. In a weird way, this is helping. Like virtual therapy."

And I needed a little therapy. Yahoo Answers wasn't cutting it lately.

"Awesome." She kissed my cheek. "I'm heading out to meet Josh for pizza, but if you need me, call or text."

"I'm good," I promised. "But maybe smell Josh's hair for me. He so looks like the kind of guy who has amazing smelling hair."

"I am not smelling his hair!" Paige picked up a small pillow and tossed it at me.

"Fine." I sighed dramatically as she spent all of three minutes to change, twist her hair into a gorgeous hairstyle, and slip on some heels.

"Bye, girls," she called out before disappearing into the hall.

As soon as the front door closed, I geared up and told myself I could do this. My chance at a real Hot Cakes shake depended on it. I gently patted my cheeks and looked at the next question on the screen.

5. **What five things would you save if your house were on fire?** My favorite picture of my parents on their wedding day. My dad's first guitar, which I can't play *anywhere* near as well as he can, but love so, so much. My Bible. The quilt Aunt Kit made me before I went off to college. My three favorite umbrellas.

I almost typed, *The napkin Dillon wrote "I Love You" on before he said the words out loud,* but quickly stopped myself.

I moved on to the second part of the questionnaire.

About Dating and Relationships: Five Questions
(We know, we know. You wouldn't be doing this right now if you were sharing a single piece of spaghetti with your guy Lady and the Tramp *style. Tell us how the dating scene has been for you! We want to know!)*

Okay. I dipped a chip. Here we go.

1. **How many serious romantic relationships have you had?** two.

2. **Do you believe in love at first sight?** Kind of, yeah. I think that at first sight you can get a "whoa, that is someone special" kind of feeling. And then love can grow out of that. But I'm a crazy hopeless romantic.

3. **How long ago did your last relationship end?** Four weeks. And also four days. It's kind of a long story.

4. **Do you think people who are dating should also be friends?** I think that would be ideal. But I've never really dated anyone who was also, as they say, "my best friend." Wish I could say I did.

5. **What do you think of people who are friends becoming romantic?** I think that could work if you hadn't put each other in the friend zone for too long. It might be pretty amazing.

Bonus Question: Is there anything we should know about that we didn't ask? Yes. I'm supremely unlucky. For example, my friend's phone was one of the ones that exploded. But not until I happened to be using it. And that kind of thing happens all the time.

I looked over my answers, skimmed the Terms and Conditions, and clicked the button at the bottom that said *Submit Application.*

Are you sure? A pop-up asked.

Not really, I thought.

But I clicked *Yes.*

"Well." I gently set the laptop on my nightstand. "I hope my answers were worth a hundred bucks."

Ding. Ding. Ding. Ding, my phone chimed.

I perked up when I saw that Aunt Kit was calling my cell.

"Hey!" I answered immediately.

"Pack a bag," Kit said without preamble.

I instantly felt warm and relieved. Aunt Kit's farmhouse in Cle Elum—about an hour and a half east of Seattle—is a beautiful B&B that has been a haven for me since I was a kid. When I begged my vagabond, camper-dwelling parents to let me spend my high school summers there. When Dillon broke up with me the first time. When I lost the job I had worked so hard to get. Staying at the Barn Quilt B&B—amid all the furniture my late Uncle Nelson made for Aunt Kit and the country chic décor she has a serious knack for—is like getting a warm hug.

My life is in Seattle—my work, my home, my friends. But Cle Elum is my refuge. And I've been in need of refuge quite a bit lately.

"You're an angel, Kit."

"We'll take care of you," Kit said.

"We?"

"The Pine Needlers are coming over tonight to make plans for Quilting for a Cause."

"Is it that time already?" I asked, referring to the huge charity event Kit's four-women-strong quilt group participates in each year.

"It is!" Kit trilled.

"Why aren't you meeting tomorrow after Big Breakfast like usual?"

"Don't tell me you forgot," Kit said, sounding slightly suspicious.

"Forgot what?"

"Um. Just that tomorrow is Lauren and Ian's engagement dinner, and I need to focus on *that* after Big Breakfast."

"That's right . . . Ian's engagement dinner." I looked over at my bulletin board. There was the very classy, very Lauren—who, granted, I've never actually met, but I think you can learn a lot from a Pinterest board—engagement announcement.

It was quite the coup that Ian, Cle Elum's golden boy, had chosen Kit's B&B over any other venue in or near town. Kit was taking it *very* seriously.

"I promised him weeks ago that I'd make sure you were there." She paused for effect. "Because he asked me to."

"He did not," I said, embarrassed at the familiar, fifteen-year-old girl crushing on the cute seventeen-year-old boy tingles.

"Oh, but he did." She stretched the word *did* into about five syllables. "Be safe."

Chapter Four

H i, sweetheart." Kit took me into a huge hug the second I walked through the door. Then she grabbed my duffle bag, got me situated on the center cushion of the couch in the large, tucked away sitting room in the back of the old farmhouse, and covered me in one of her award-winning quilts before disappearing to fix me the comfort meal she's been making me since I was a kid: a grilled cheese sandwich with mayonnaise instead of butter.

I smiled at her back and looked out at the sun as it began to set behind the tall pine trees that framed the large clearing behind the B&B . . .

Aunt Kit has always been so good to me. She wasn't able to have children. And I grew up with parents who weren't big on security or structure, which I, nerd that I am, actually kind of craved. So when I talked them into letting me move out of the camper and in with Aunt Kit those summers when I was in high school, it was like it was meant to be. And secretly, I relished the mandatory mealtimes, the eleven o'clock curfew, the smelling my breath when I got home. And, of course, The Pine Needlers teasing me about the time I was spending at the Irish Rose Inn.

Ian O'Connell's family's inn.

Now tonight, just over ten years later, there they were: The Pine Needlers. Kit. Kit's two best friends since elementary school (and extra B&B hands) Lizette Moore-Fiefer and her younger sister, Annie Moore-Thompson. Lacey Freeland was missing, but that was because she had just had a baby. She, of course, got a surprise baby quilt from the rest of the PNs and it was adorable.

Lizette handed me a mug of cocoa and plunked down beside me. "That horrible, horrible periodontist," she said. "Breaking up with you with someone he met in Morocco. The nerve!"

Lizette loves gossip. Which is kind of dangerous because she NEVER remembers details correctly. Naturally, she runs Cle Elum's busiest hair salon.

"I have something for you," Annie said, quickly hopping up from her spot on the floor and grabbing her quilted purse—which I swear is like Mary Poppins's bag. She pulled out a pumpkin carving knife and a neon pink ace bandage before retrieving a bag filled with stones. "Here. These are healing crystals. You're supposed to put the white one near your heart." She stuffed a clear white rock down my bra. "Well, maybe two for safety." And another one went in.

Annie is a retired school teacher who has a new passion every week. She's been a club DJ in the city (DJ Quilt Pain). A notary public. And if the thing she wants to do requires a pricy certification, she goes for the bargain replacement: Massage Careapy. Cosmeticsology. Zomba. (Zumba with zombie-like dance moves.)

"Crystals aren't going to do anything," Lizette said with a roll of her blue eyes. "What we need to do is make a list of all the eligible bachelors in town. There's this new guy at the paper. I actually snapped a picture of him today." She searched her bag for her phone.

Lizette has a weekly column in the local newspaper. It's mostly just a place for her to gossip and an outlet to talk about her life while referring to herself as "a friend of mine."

"If she believes, the universe will provide," Annie— who has shorter hair, shorter nails, and a four inches shorter frame than her sister—said with a nod.

"I can go out in the yard and pick up rocks that are more powerful than those ridiculous crystals!" Lizette retorted.

One thing I can always count on is Lizette and Annie's sibling rivalry. I told you. They're competitive when it comes to everything. Grades in extension school classes. DMV vision tests.

Though I've never seen it as bad as it was in May at the Mid Washington Quilt Show when their quilts got the *exact same score.*

Suddenly, there were rumors flying:

Annie used a machine on a part of her quilt that she said she did by hand! Shameful!

Lizette did not *tea dye the part of the quilt she said she did!* Outrageous!

Annie was seen in a seedy skateboard park handing a local seamstress a wad of cash a week before the show! Scandalous!

"You two." Kit handed me my sandwich, complete with four pickle spears. "Okay, Boodle,"—that's the short version of her nickname for me; we're Kit and Caboodle—"Tell us everything."

I relayed the whole sad tale, complete with the Hipster BBQ song that was stuck in my head and my break-through moment when I realized just how much Dillon uses the word . . . *bruh*.

"I bet I can find some karma rocks," Annie offered intensely.

"I can offer him a free haircut," Lizette said competitively, "and then I can do this—" She flashed a photo on her phone of a guy with tufts of hair sticking out of his head at random. It was on a site called Seemed Like a Good Idea or something like that.

Lizette loves that kind of stuff. Like Fail Blog and Awkward Family Photos. And that Jimmy Fallon's Bad Signs bit.

I nibbled on my sandwich, feeling comforted as my Cle Elum family rallied around me. It had been a while since I'd been back—what with all the job applying and life failing—and it felt good.

"Actually, Gabby," Kit curled her silk pajama-clad legs up under her, so fully at home in Uncle Nelson's big, comfy chair. "I think I know just what you need."

"What?"

"To help us come up with some Quilting for a Cause ideas."

"Yeah," Annie put in. "Ninety-nine percent of people who did some act of service when feeling down felt better afterwards."

I smiled. I loved how whenever Annie isn't totally sure about a statistic, she just says ninety-nine percent.

"Sounds good to me." I rested my head on the couch.

I've been an honorary member of The Pine Needlers since I was about ten. Even though sixteen years later I'm still at about the same skill level. Now knitting? That is definitely more my thing.

"All right," Kit said, "This year the Quilting for a Cause Super Saturday—where every quilt group comes to show what they've done—is the first Saturday in December. So I'm thinking whatever we do should culminate the Saturday after Thanksgiving."

"That sounds perfect," Lizette said, and Annie agreed.

Lizette flipped my hair into twists and braids as she said, "I think we should do quilts for the fire station. We haven't done that since 2014. And this past summer so many of them went down to fight those fires in California."

"That's a good idea," Annie put in. "I also kind of like Project Linus. I love that those quilts go to kids in need."

"I was thinking we might like to try something totally new this year," Aunt Kit said. "I read about this group called Quilts of Honor. They give quilts to military veterans. They call them Quilted Hugs of Gratitude. Isn't that neat?"

Goosebumps suddenly covered my arms.

"How about Kindness Quilts?" I said.

All three women focused on me.

"Kindness Quilts," Lizette said. "What are those?"

"Well." I hopped up and grabbed Kit's iPad from the side table. "I don't think they're a thing. But maybe we can make them one."

I clicked away on the iPad. "Paige has this supremely awesome patient named Lennox. She does this online project called Project Good Little Anything."

I pulled up the blog on the tablet and all the ladies gathered around to read the screen.

After showing them the Homepage I clicked on *How to Participate.*

Step 1: If you do something kind or see something kind—literally anything, from smiling at someone in the crazy long line at Walgreens to going on a relief trip to Honduras—make a note of it. (Mental, paper, or electronic.)

Step 2: Memorialize your kind thing—via your own blog, FB, Twitter, Insta, etc.,—and email me a link (or include the hashtag #projectgoodlittleanything), and I'll do everything I can to post the goodness right here.

Step 3: Bask in the joy of sending (or receiving) true kindness. Best feeling ever, I've got to admit!!

*May I kindly ask that you keep it all PG. We have seven-year-old readers here, dudes. If you can't keep it tame for the kidlets, then, well, good on you for doing something, but I'm gonna internet bleep you, just sayin'.

Now . . . Go! Let's be the good guys in people's stories!

Love and hugs and red Jolly Ranchers for all,
Lennox

"I love her writing voice," Lizette said to me. "I mean, from one writer to another, I'm very impressed by . . . the fluidity . . . and her use of iambic . . . pedometer."

"Shh!" Annie, who was still reading, shot Lizette a growly look.

"You can never let me have a moment, can you, Annie?"

"So what are you thinking?" Kit asked me, after allowing enough time for reading. "We make quilts and do something kind with them?"

"Actually," I got up and started to scribble on the whiteboard used during most quilt group meetings. "I'm thinking the quilts should be made from good deeds. Like, we do simple—yet beautiful—block quilts, and every quilt square represents a good deed done. And a record of the good deeds that went into each quilt can be attached somehow."

"We can make little booklets that go with each quilt," Lizette suggested. "I saw this company on TV that makes handbags that include the story of who made them in a cool little booklet."

"I like that!" I said, excitement rising in my voice. "Each quilt comes with a story of kindness."

"And then we can auction off the quilts," Annie suggested.

"Yes!" I pointed at her. "And buying the quilt at auction could be the final good deed."

"It could even be giving the quilt away," Annie said with a shrug.

The ideas just started flowing after that.

"We can donate the auction money to Seattle Pediatric Hospital," I said.

"We could have the auction here," Kit offered. "A silent auction with the quilts displayed and yummy food and fun music."

"I could run an article in the paper," Lizette offered, "asking people in the community to join us in the challenge and even with making the quilts."

"I could start a Facebook page and have the whole community start recording their good deeds." Annie offered. "And I could ask this Lennox girl if she's fine if we use the name she already created."

Everyone nodded and agreed, excitement filling the air.

"Let's start with a goal of six quilts," Kit suggested.

"That means if we go the safe route and use twelve-inch blocks," Lizette said. "We'll need thirty good deeds per quilt. So 180 total over the course of six weeks."

"We can do better than that!" I put in. Even though, if I'm one hundred percent honest, most of the numbers were kind of going over my head.

"Do you want to try more quilts or more blocks?" Kit asked.

"Both!" I said.

Right here all I heard was a bunch of numbers being thrown out by each of the women.

Then Kit raised her hand all officially and said, "Okay. We're going to make eight quilts. With ten-inch blocks. So forty-eight blocks per quilt. That means we have a little less than two months to do 384 Good Little Anythings."

"We can totally pull that off," Lizette said.

"Agreed," Annie put in, with a smile at her sister.

"Oh my gosh, you guys," I said. "I can't believe this is really happening! I can't wait to talk to Lennox!"

"Thanks for the great idea," Kit said, hugging my shoulders.

"I think it must be meant to be," I said as I squeezed her hand. "Oh wait! Look! Lennox just posted a new video."

"Good Friday, friends!" I read aloud from the post that contained a link to a YouTube video. "We're going to start this weekend off right with this amazing video from the Helaman Halls dorms at Brigham Young University. Be good, good guys!"

"Play it!" Lizettte said.

"I can get it to play on the TV," Annie offered.

"That sounds great," Lizette and I said in unision.

And after a bit of toggling, the video was on the big screen TV. We all got situated and watched.

A song started to play, all acoustic guitar and pretty voices singing in harmony.

Then, as the music played, people held up posters with black Sharpie messages written on them.

A group of apparent freshmen dorm-dwellers, in a common room with couches and a few vending machines, were first.

Their poster read: *Have I done any good in the world today?*

Next came posters being held by a beautiful variety of people.

I'm pretty sure all of our eyes were blurred with "uplifting video" tears after the first few minutes.

A little kid wearing a backwards baseball cap: *There's this boy in my class who gets left out when we're playing catch at recess. So one day when I was a team captain, I picked him first. He smiled soooo big.*

A guy wearing a suit: *I asked my grandma to tell me how she met my grandpa. And I really listened.*

A teenager with a skateboard propped against his leg: *Math has always been hard for me. But last year I had this teacher who helped me really get it. I'm applying to BYU this spring, and I want to be an engineer. I wrote that teacher a Thank You note the other day.*

A three year old girl: *I drew my auntie a picture of Jesus and hung it in her hospital room when she had to have a hysterectomy.*

A woman with a pink scarf on her head: *At first, when I lost my hair during cancer treatment, I always wore wigs. But then, one day, I went to the grocery store with a scarf. A woman came up to me, with tears in her eyes, and told me she had just started treatment, and seeing me in my scarf had taken away some of her trepidation over losing her hair. A wig does me good. But that scarf did so much more.*

Then the students were back: *Have anyone's burdens been lightened today?*

An elderly man holding the hands of two tween girls: *My angels came to sing to me.*

At the bottom, there was a note in different writing: *Our grandpa has Alzheimer's. He doesn't recognize us when we come to sing to him every Sunday, but he calls us his angels.*

Two Cub Scouts standing next to a man with a tattoo on his left arm: *Last Veteran's Day, we took a picture with this man who stood on an overpass and saluted the US flag all day. He said he plans to do it again this year.*

A man with grey hair: *Someone put beautiful flowers on my wife's gravestone.*

A woman who looked about thirty: *I got my car, filled with my four kids, stuck in the snow, and two guys in basketball shorts got out of their car and helped me dig free.*

A woman with pain in her eyes: *A new friend remembered my birthday and brought by a loaf of bread.*

And then the last poster, held by all in the video, sent something through me I'd never quite experienced before.

"And the King shall answer and say unto them, Verily I say unto you, Insamuch as ye have done it unto one of the least of these my brethren, ye have done it unto me."

Matthew 25:40

A sweet silence filled the room. Then Aunt Kit said, "We have to do this."

"All in favor?" Lizette said softly.

"Needle eye," we all said in unision.

"See you tomorrow morning!" Aunt Kit stood at the back door and waved good-bye to Annie and Lizette.

"Bright and early!" Lizette promised.

"Expecting any guests tonight?" I asked Kit as she closed the door.

"No reservations," she said. "But there's a wedding at Ritter Farms, so we might get some for Big Breakfast tomorrow. I had Max drive over there since I figured a wedding means lots of eligible—"

Max is the handyman at the B&B. Well, handy*kid*. He's saving up for college. "Lots of eligible what?" I asked.

Kit simply bolted the front door and flicked her eyes, which definitely had a little twinkle in them, toward me.

"Well. Since you're—" She stopped abruptly at the sound of her phone alarm.

"Since I'm what?"

"Never mind!" She made a shooing motion with her hands. "Come on! It's time to watch *Wheel.*"

Every weeknight Kit watches *Wheel of Fortune* in her master bedroom.

I quickly booked it to the room, where I sat on a chair in the small seating alcove, and fought the urge to chew on my lower lip, my preferred nervous habit.

Why was I nervous for a little primetime game show fun?

Because Kit is serious about a few things in life: the B&B, her family, And *Wheel of Fortune.*

When *Wheel* is on, Kit takes her normally, well, *normal,* level of rule enforcement to a whole new, dare I say, ca-razy, level.

Here are the *Wheel Watcher's Rules:*

1. DO NOT guess the puzzle out loud before she does. If you dare, get ready for a little passive aggressive dig. Like "Gabby, I never realized how much bigger your left ear is than your right ear."
2. When the prize puzzle comes up DO NOT guess where the person is going before Kit does.
3. If you are watching *Wheel* you are watching *Wheel.* You are not talking, reading, or eating *anything* that makes any noise including but not limited to chips, licorice, and pudding.
4. Don't comment on Vanna's dress. Or on Pat's hair.

5. And this is kind of a weird one: don't comment on how no one ever wins the car. Apparently the *Wheel* is perfect and untouchable.

I sat motionless as Cat Sajak, Kit's calico, who spends his whole day in Kit's master suite, jumped onto my lap.

The first "Toss-Up" category was "Person."

The puzzle board read:

__AD__ GA__A

Kit was shouting, "Mady Gaba! Lady Gana! Katy Ganja!"

But I didn't dare speak.

I just sat there, still as a wax figure.

Luckily, I made it through the half hour without any infractions.

And then it was me and Kit.

"Now it's Kit and Caboodle time." She hopped up and filled a tray of with her famous scones and raspberry jam, and pretty glass jars filled with treats she'd obviously bought just for me: Doritos, Laffy Taffy, and my favorite kinds of Corn Nuts.

Then we hung out on Kit's big, fluffy four-poster bed and watched a Meg Ryan and Tom Hanks movie marathon that was on TV. Kit rubbed my head and listened as I cried about how *I* wasn't just *sleepless* in Seattle, I was also houseless, jobless, and bra-that-actually-fits-less.

I fell asleep sometime around midnight. Kit gently roused me and led me up to the room in the attic where I always sleep when I come to visit. All around the room she had left me little gifts: new socks, a pack of pens, and notes with corny inspirational sayings that she knew would make me laugh.

I drifted off on the soft, warm bed covered with one of my favorite of Kit's quilts, feeling happy and hopeful.

The last thought I remember having was *I'm going to see Ian tomorrow.*

Chapter Five

I slept better than I had in ages.

Somehow, in the warm cocoon that was the bed in my attic bedroom at the Barn Quilt B&B—which is named for the large painted quilt replica on the barn— for just a moment, I forgot about everything. I forgot about Dillon and his new girlfriend who I was somehow totally sure did not own a pair of pumps whose right heel was being held on by chewing gum. I forgot about how not psychic I am. I forgot about how I have no idea when or even *if* I'll get to teach again. I forgot about how I went to the Pampered Pets going-out-of-business sale to see if any of the ninety percent-off pet clothes would fit me.

And, as I forgot the bad, I was suddenly awash in the good. The refreshing feeling of a full night of sleep, uninterrupted by the sound of Iris playing video games with teenagers in Finland and passing fire trucks. The soft crispness of the sheets Kit puts on all the B&B beds. The incredible smell of The Barn Quilt's famous Saturday

"Big Breakfast"—pancakes, sausage, cinnamon rolls, etc.—wafting up to the attic.

And then my phone rang.

I stretched my arms to the sky, completely relaxed. Then I just slid under the covers and ignored it.

But it rang again.

I pushed one arm out of my cocoon and snapped it up from the nightstand. It was my mom.

"Hey, Mom," I said, my voice still froggy from sleep.

"Oh my sweet little bird!" she cried. "Are you okay? It went to voicemail. Kit said you were doing just awful. And then you didn't answer. I was freaking out!"

"Ah," I said, suddenly realizing. "Kit called you."

"Yes she called me! I'm your mother! She thought I should know that my daughter has hit rock bottom."

"I haven't hit rock bottom," I said.

But she didn't seem to hear me. "This is all that awful doctor's fault! You know that doctors learn in medical school to turn off their feelings. There's a secret class they have to take that teaches them. They take an oath. I think it's like 'We are doctors. We are robots. We are doctors. We are robots.' And it just repeats like that."

"I'm fine, Mom." I closed my eyes. "Kit is taking care of me."

"Oh." Mom paused for effect. "I'm glad your aunt is taking such good care of you that you don't need me at all."

"Oh, Mom, of course I need you."

"It's okay," Mom said. "It's your journey. I . . .," she made a dramatic sigh, "understand. And I really am so sorry, love child." My mom calls me this as a term of endearment. I don't think she realizes what she's saying.

"I know, Mom."

Three. Two. One—

"Although . . . I never did like him for you. For him to say that I obviously didn't have gangrene in my foot if it was cured by a guy in a van with high quality patchouli oil? That was just disrespectful."

I nodded, instantly remembering their first meeting. "I know. I know."

"Here honeysuckle, your dad wants to say hi."

"Hi!" My dad's sweet, gentle voice came onto the line.

"Hi, Dad. I miss you guys."

"Say something encouraging, Rock." My mom's voice was muffled. She thinks putting her hand on the bottom of the phone effectively mutes her voice.

"Like what?" My dad asked.

"I don't know. She just got her heart broken. Her fancy education is going down the toilet. And that fertility stick I gave her is only going to work for so long. Say something nice."

"Cheer up, buttercup."

That's my dad. The guitarist of few words who snuck me Pop Tarts when I was a kid—and told me that no, the red stuff inside was not alien guts, like my mom told me—taught me everything I know about bluffing in poker, and gave me my eclectic love for pretty much every kind of music.

"Okay," Mom said. "We better go. We've already put more than enough radiation into the world today. I'll have to do 500 sit ups to counteract it."

"Of course," I said like it made total sense. "Thanks for calling, Mom. Love you both."

"Kisses and hugs," Mom said. "We're going to start heading your way. Kit told me what you came up with for the big Quilting for a Cause event and I'd love to be there to see how it comes together."

"That sounds great. Love you guys. Be safe. Check in when you can." I hung up with a smile. Kooky as they were, they were great parents, who always let me know they loved me.

My phone buzzed with a text. From Lizette. I frowned as I read it.

Good Morning Sunshine! You coming down to Big Breakfast?

Still getting ready, I texted back. *Pretty soon.*

I took my time in the cozy bathroom just outside the bedroom, and when I was sufficiently spiffed and dressed in the vintage red dress I'd brought for the engagement party, I went downstairs.

The big, open kitchen and dining area was abuzz, as always, for Big Breakfast. The gorgeous twenty-seat reclaimed wood dining table and various seating areas in the space were filled with late-arrival B&B guests, Kit's friends, and of course, a spattering of Cle Elum's colorful residents.

"Hey, Boodle." Kit greeted me in the kitchen, where she and the B&B cook—a girl name Mallory who, like the handyman, was saving up for college—were busy making the farm fresh meal. Kit kissed me on the cheek, her hands busy with pancake batter. "Sleep well?"

"Better than I have in forever." I plucked a few blueberries from a colander and popped one into my mouth. "I need to do something to repay you for everything."

"Gabby! There you are." Lizette licked her finger and wiped something from my cheek. "Grab your breakfast and go sit at the end of the table."

"What?"

She motioned with her chin. "Over there."

"Okay . . ." I grabbed a plate and began filling it to the brim.

"What are you?" Lizette asked as she removed half my food. "A truck driver?"

I frowned at her.

"You can get seconds if you want."

"Okay . . ." I bit into a piece of bacon as I started to move away.

"Wait." Lizette grabbed my shoulders and pulled on my lips like she was a dental assistant. "When did you get your braces off?"

"When I was thirteen."

"Well," she moved her head really close to my mouth. "Your teeth look almost normal. All the better."

"Thanks?"

"Come on." Lizette grabbed me and steered me to the dining room. "There's a spot for you at the end of the table."

I looked at her in confusion as she pulled out a chair and pushed on my head like a cop helping an arrestee into the back of a cruiser. I should have known from the twitch in her nose that she was up to something.

Then, three bites into my breakfast, a guy I didn't recognize pulled out the chair across from mine.

"Hey," he said. "Anyone sitting here?"

I looked up and down the massive table. Since I'd come down as things were starting to wind down, there were plenty of open seats. "Nope."

"I was told this is where I should sit."

The guy took a seat and pushed up the sleeves of his grey v-neck sweater before cutting into his pancakes. He was really good looking in a spends-a-lot-of-time-in-front-of-the-mirror way. He was just barely tall with chiseled arms and hair that did that swoopy thing that's in for guys' hair right now.

"So who told you to sit there exactly?" I took a gulp of Kit's fresh-squeezed grapefruit juice and looked for Lizette, who had suddenly made herself scarce.

"Someone official." His eyes were glued to his phone. "I'm Jason."

"Gabby," I introduced myself. "Do you live around here?"

"Nope." He slipped the phone into his pocket. "Just visiting."

"Oh," I said as I nibbled on a strawberry. "Did you stay here last night?"

"Nah. I stayed over in Roslyn. My buddy is getting married at Ritter Farms. A bunch of us are staying at the Pineview Inn and the lady at the front desk had a bunch of these breakfast coupons out, so I thought, hey, free food."

"What coupons?" I leaned forward like I misunderstood him. The guy pulled a cardstock coupon from his jeans pocket. He flicked it at me like it was a paper throwing-star. It nearly hit me in the eye.

I recovered and read the coupon.

Come to Big Breakfast this Saturday at The Barn Quilt B&B in Cle Elum. Guys Eat Free! From 11 a.m.–12 p.m. All you can eat! Pancakes! Meats! Must present this coupon! Non-Transferable.

"Oh my gosh." I snapped my head to kitchen, where Kit, Lizette, and Annie—who were all watching—immediately pretended to be busy. Kit putting already done pancakes on the griddle, Lizette arranging toothpicks, and Annie looking at her elbows.

"So." Jason looked over at me. "I *was* thinking bridesmaid. But, you're pretty cute. What are you doing tonight?"

"Well. I'm—"

"I'm actually gonna stop you right there," Jason said, holding up his hand.

"I'm sorry?"

"Before this can happen, I need to know your numbers."

"What kind of—"

"First." Jason held up a finger. "Your age."

"Twenty-six," I answered.

"Good." Jason nodded. "Gotta have that two at the beginning."

I frowned. "How old are yo—"

"Second," Jason said before I could get in a word. "How often do you go out of the house wearing clothes that only girls think are cute?"

"Um . . ." I looked down at my dress. "I own an umbrella hat, so . . ."

"Ooh." Jason winced dramatically as his eyes settled on a pretty redhead in the buffet line, like he was already gearing up for what was next. "But. Hey. The last number is more important."

"What's the last number?"

"Your credit score."

Oh. Um . . .

"Well. I'm guessing not that great since nearly every ad on my Facebook page is some version of *Low Credit? We'll Fix It! Need Cash? We've Got It!* But—"

I was just about to attempt to change the subject when Jason's phone buzzed.

He looked down at a text and abruptly stood. "Wedding nonsense." He upped his chin at me and knocked his knuckles on the table. "Be good, Kathy. Maybe I'll find you if I get bored."

As soon as he was out the door, Kit and Lizette appeared at my side.

"What did you think?" Lizette was smiling.

"I know you guys mean well, but free breakfast coupons?" I buried my head in my hands.

"Gabby." Annie casually sidled up to us. "Can you go get me something from the front room?"

"Sure," I said as I draped a napkin over my plate. "What do you need?"

"Just whatever you think I might like," Annie said.

Then she linked arms with Kit and Lizette and the three scurried away.

I took a deep breath and slowly made my way to the front room. There I found a guy with dark wavy hair that was neatly parted on the side of his head with what appeared to be a lot of mousse or gel or something. He was wearing a light blue polo shirt with jeans and tennis shoes. He kind of looked like Ray Romano.

"Gabby?" He said when he saw me.

"That's me." I waved.

I looked over my shoulder and saw my little trio of cupids watching from behind not at all obvious cookie sheets as the two of us sat down on the window seat.

"I'm Joe," the man said, reaching out a hand politely.

"Hi, Joe," I said with a nervous smile.

"You have a beautiful smile, Gabby" he said.

"Thank you."

"So your aunt owns this place?"

I nodded.

His phone blared a rap song.

"I'm so sorry. I forgot to turn that off." Joe checked the screen. "Oh wait. It's my mom. Do you mind?"

"Not at all." I made a waving motion. "Go ahead."

"Hey Mom. The breakfast was wonderful. In fact, it just got better. I'm talking to a very lovely young lady. "

He was silent for a minute, and I grabbed a nearby magazine and flipped through the pages.

"Hmm? Oh. Let's see." He looked over at me. "I'd say a seven or eight. Maybe even a nine with a little TLC."

Um. Did she just ask him to *rate* me?

"I'll ask her. Gabby, do you cook?"

Hmm. A few days ago, I made a baked potato with expired relish on it for dinner. "I'm learning."

"She said she's learning," Joe said into the phone. "I guess not everyone can be you. All right. Talk to you soon." He set his phone on the table. "Aren't moms just the best?"

"They sure are."

He smiled. "So you're big on family?"

"Most important thing in the world."

"That's great." Joe shook his head. "I can't tell you how many times I've started talking to a young lady who practically runs the other way when I whip out the photos of my family."

I frowned. "Really? That's too bad."

Joe reached back into his pocket for his phone. "You want to see some?"

"Sure." I held out my hand.

I was expecting pictures of him and his parents, some siblings, maybe some nieces and nephews.

But all the photos were of him and his mom. Riding a tandem bike. Pedaling on a pedal boat.

"So you and your mom and pretty close, huh?" I asked, staring at a pic of them sitting in a sauna together.

Joe nodded. "She still sews my name into all my clothes."

"Oh," I said in the most casual voice I could manage.

"Gabby?" I looked behind me and saw a guy I was almost sure I recognized. He was edgy, with a motorcycle jacket and lots of chin scruff. "I'm sorry, but we need you out back."

"Oh." I got up. "Okay."

I gave Joe a weak wave before heading through the front room, dining room, and out onto the deck.

"What's . . ." I turned around on the deck a few times, not spotting any need.

"You looked kind of trapped," the guy in the motor-cycle jacket said. "I just thought I'd help out."

"Thanks." I grabbed a bottle of orange juice off the glass deck table and twisted the top off. Where did I know him from? And why when I thought about his name did

I think Pork? No one is named Pork. Well. Maybe some Kardashian.

"Not a problem." He reached out and touched my forearm.

I narrowed my eyes. "I swear I know you, but I don't know how."

"We met once," the guy said. Then I saw his eyes flick to something behind me, and I looked over my shoulder just in time to see Lizette giving him the thumbs up.

And that's when the synapses fired in my brain and I realized it was Lizette's friend Marlow's nephew, whose family lives in Lakedale (not too far from Cle Elum). I'd met him at Kit's Christmas Party last year, and we'd debated about the best kind of cranberry sauce. He was a cool guy. One hundred percent not my type, but still a cool guy. He rode a motorcycle. Wanted to be famous. Wore skinnier jeans than I did. I'm pretty sure I followed him on Instagram. Or was it Twitter?

I used to be a social media abstainer. Then I went to this job seminar and the instructor said you never know where you'll get a job lead and he told us to friend everyone and heart and like everything. So now I do. Who knows if it really helps?

"I'm Gabby," I said.

"I remember," the guy said with a mischievous smile. "Do you remember my name?"

I took a sip of my juice.

"Nicely played." He laughed. "It's Roarke."

"That's right. Roarke the actor. How's the actor's life?"

"Awesome." Roarke stood up straighter. "I think I'm getting close to my big break. Last month I booked a job as Guy Holding a Ballpoint Pen for a commercial. And starting next spring, I will be the crew sock guy on all Hawks socks packages."

"Wow." I smiled at his self-deprecating humor.

"I actually have an audition for a movie that's filming here in Washington," he added. "That's more or less why I'm here."

"I hope it goes well."

"Thanks." He looked down at something in his left hand. "So. What's life like in the bank business?"

"I'm sorry?"

"I just . . . I heard that you're a teller these days."

"From who?" I frowned.

He shrugged. "I don't remember. But enough about work. How's, um, sheet?"

"Sheet?" I asked, not sure I understood him correctly.

"Yeah." He looked at his hand again. "What's it like living with someone with such an interesting name?"

"What name?"

"Never mind." Roarke squinted, his eyes focused on his left palm.

"What are you looking at?" I moved toward him.

"Nothing." He quickly moved his left arm behind him and slipped his hand into his pocket and kept his arm there. "So, um, I heard you like umpires."

"Huh?"

"Nothing better than a good, square-shaped umpire."

"What on earth are you talking about?" I sort of lunged toward him, only this time I was quicker and I caught a glimpse of a piece of paper he was reading from.

I snapped it out of his hand.

There, in Lizette's hard to read cursive, was this list:

Gabby is a bank teller.

She lives in Seattle with her friend from college—I think her name is Sheet.

She collects umbrellas.

"Unbelievable," I said.

"I'm sorry." Roarke held his hands up. "Your aunt promised me five free nights here at the B&B. And I'm a broke actor."

"Wow," I said with a laugh. "Five free nights? I wouldn't have turned that down either."

"Bank telling doesn't a millionaire make?"

I closed my eyes and shook my head.

"Not a bank teller?" he said.

"A fortune teller."

"And your roommate is not named Sheet?"

"Paige."

Roarke laughed.

"And the umpire thing?" He looked confused.

I pointed at the list. "Dude. That says *umbrellas.* I collect umbrellas."

"Wow." Roarke's eyes got kind of wide. "I sure blew that one."

"No you didn't," I said. "That list is, just, well, it's Lizette. She's a great talker. But not so much with the listening. Or the remembering."

"Well then *you* tell me." He was smooth. The kind of smooth that could get a girl in trouble.

"I'm a fortune teller, like I said, I live with my roommate, Paige, and, well, the umbrella thing."

"A fortune teller sounds cooler than a bank teller."

"Actually. I'm a teacher. Currently on permanent unpaid leave."

"I guess this is a good time to tell you," Roarke said. "I lied before. I didn't get the Hawks crew sock. I got the ankle sock."

"Well we're two sad people, aren't we?" I said.

"I bet you I'm sadder," Roarke said.

"I'll take that bet."

"You're on." Roarke rasied his eyebrows. "Loser buys dinner."

Ah. Nice move. "As long as by 'dinner' you mean a hot dog and drink at Costco."

"That works," Roarke said. Then he flashed me that dangerous smile.

"Okay." I sat down on one of the patio chairs. "I have a collection of hairbands that are actually the rubber bands from stalks of broccoli."

"I can't afford Xbox Live," Roarke said as he sat across from me, "so I give the kid across the hall girl advice and he lets me play on his account."

"The other day, I saw a teenager drop a jumbo pretzel on the floor at the mall, and he just left it there. So I yelled, 'five second rule' and dove for it."

"Whoa," Roarke whistled. "You don't mess around."

"Nope." I crossed my arms in front of me as if to say, *you had enough, punk?*

Roarke upped his chin. "I got a free movie pass for filling out a survey. And I ate the tub of popcorn I found left under my seat. Plus about fifteen Milk Duds that were in the cup holder."

"Whoa." I blinked a few times.

"Sounds like I'm pulling ahead," Roarke said.

"No . . . I've gotta have something . . ." I snapped my fingers. "I . . . dang it . . . I—"

"For my mom's birthday," Roarke said quickly. "I dug through the boxes in the garage and gave her a macaroni jewelry box I made in elementary school. She oohed and aahed and told me how great a job I did on it."

"I massaged my roommate Iris's bunions in exchange for a cup of her Honey Nut Cheerios!"

"I was trying to sell solar panels in a nice neighborhood when I saw these kids selling lemonade for a quarter. I went to buy a cup and I saw there were like five $20 bills in the tip jar. So . . ."

My mouth fell open. "You didn't."

"No." He closed his eyes and shook his head. "You'd have to be truly evil to rob a kid's lemonade stand."

I sighed. "Thank goodness."

"But . . ."

"But?" My eyebrows shot up. "There's a but in that story?"

"I opened a competing lemonade stand right across the street. I made nearly two hundred bucks."

"You win." I wanted to laugh, but felt really wrong about it. "I can't beat that."

"Hello, sweetie." Lizette sat next to me and slid a pancake into the shape of a heart onto the table. "How are you?"

"Just talking about how poor we are," I said.

"Don't talk about that." Lizette brushed my hair behind my ears. "Talk about how great you are at playing the harp."

I've never touched a harp in my life. "You mean the harmonica?"

"No . . ." Lizette looked confused.

"Hey Gabby." Kit gripped the back of my chair. "Can I steal you?"

"Um." I looked at Roarke. "Okay."

Roarke reached for his phone in his pocket. "Whoa. Is it really already noon? I better get going." He handed me his business card and then stood up. "Give me a call and we'll get that hot dog."

"Sounds good." I gave him a little wave as he headed inside and grabbed a motorcycle helmet from the breakfast bar on the way out.

Kit took me into the kitchen.

"So." Annie accosted me. "Did you enjoy any certain conversations you had this morning?"

"Well . . ." I began.

"We'll talk about that later." Kit cut me off, sounding frantic as she cleared some cups from the kitchen bar. "It's noon, and the engagement dinner is now going to be at *five.*"

"Oh boy," I said.

"Yeah." Kit shot me a panicked look. She was already freaking out about this dinner. Because, of all the nearby places they could have chosen, Ian O'Connell and his lifestyle blogger fiancée were coming to the Barn Quilt B&B. Now she had two less hours to make it perfect.

"Tell us what to do, Kit," Annie said.

And as Kit started to dole out assignments, there it was again, that thought: *I'm going to see Ian O'Connell.*

In five hours.

# Chapter Six

Yes, it's true.

I, Gabrielle Spring Malone, used to have a major, secret summer crush on Ian O'Connell.

It happened like this.

I'd been spending summers at the B&B for two years. Then, the summer after my sophomore year of high school, the O'Connells moved to Cle Elum from Chicago and turned the old Mayor's Mansion into the Irish Rose Inn.

Almost immediately, Kit got all territorial, which led her to

1. Begin stealth attacks on the rival inn. For example, when travelers would come into the Barn Quilt and ask, "Is this the the Irish Rose" she would answer, "Oh did you find them on bedbug finder?" Then she'd scratch her nose.

And

2. Give me the mission to check out the Irish Rose, which I, being a longtime fan of Nancy Drew, took very seriously.

I popped up in the windowsills all slow and creepy-like. I snagged two of the breakfast potato rolls and told Kit they were dry, when they were actually amazing. I peeked into the rooms. I skimmed the comments in the guest book.

Then, on day three of my mission, I literally ran into the family's seventeen-year-old son building a chicken coop. (I told him I worked for the Department of New Inns and Laundromats.)

He was the cutest boy I had ever seen in real life. He was almost a foot taller than me with muscles that came from hard work, not a gym. He had kind blue-green eyes and blond hair and eyelashes that got lighter the longer summer went on. He drove an old Ford truck. And he tossed everything that was in his hands for more than a minute into the air.

Soon we were talking every day as I helped him do work around the Irish Rose.

At first, we just talked about nothing. The weather. Sports. Current events. The fact that Ian found it crazy that people think *pizza* when they think *Chicago*, because they really should think *hot dogs*.

But then it got deeper.

Soon, even though I only saw him a few months out of the year, he was the person I told everything to.

I started with all my little secrets: I eat Cocoa Puffs for the sole purpose of drinking the chocolate milk they leave behind. My dad taught me how to play the piano and the guitar, but I would never have an ability like his to play them. I have a strange affinity for 90s rap. I get really happy when I see silver crayons. I can only drink Cherry Dr. Pepper out of a clear glass, otherwise it tastes like a penny.

And then I told him bigger secrets: how mean some kids were to me, the nerdy new kid who lived in a camper and wore thick glasses. How movies where people overcome the odds always make me cry—I think because I always root for the underdog. How I carried my Bible with me every time I had a first day at a new school. How I wanted to be a teacher when I grew up.

Ian told me some of his too: how his favorite part of Christmas in Chicago was seeing the members of the church near his house do a living Nativity. And how he was the only person in his family who went. How he wanted to be a professional baseball player. He liked to play chess with his grandpa. He couldn't tell when someone was good or bad at the drums (it all just sounded like noise to him). How he was absolutely terrified of flying.

Soon we were swinging on the swings at the elementary school, talking as we swung for hours. Hanging out at Speelyi Beach and jumping into the water together when it was warm enough. Buying handfuls of candy in Roslyn. Playing two-man baseball on the old, worn Cle Elum-Roslyn High School field.

Ian was my favorite part of summer. My first best friend.

Then on July 4, three days after I turned sixteen, something—everything—happened.

Ian was leaving for Louisville the next day. I baked him a cake that was supposed to look like a cardinal, but it looked more like Woody the Woodpecker. He gave me a t-shirt that said Irish-ish and told me it would give me luck. We watched the fireworks together in the back of Ian's truck, making ourselves sick with cake, popcorn, and the candy I got from the awesome candy shop in Roslyn.

Then, as Ian drove me home, it started raining. Hard. Ian parked in front of the B&B and opened my door for me. Then, suddenly, he grabbed my hand, and pulled me out into the downpour. We ran. And ran. Through all the spots we'd created memories over the past summer. We laughed like crazy. Our clothes stuck to our bodies. Our hair got drenched.

I'm not sure how long we'd been running when he just stopped.

And I stopped too.

Without a word, he brushed the wet hair out of my face. He stood there, out of breath, looking at me. Then he put a hand on my waist. The air between us grew heavy. I wanted to kiss him more than I wanted my next breath.

But.

Suddenly the loud sound of cracking lightning made us jump.

Ian let go of me and blinked, water falling from his eyelashes.

"I'll come by tomorrow," he said.

I nodded.

"I'm going to miss you, Nancy Drew."

He said it so finally I was scared he wouldn't come back the next day. And, though I waited, he didn't.

That was the last time I saw him.

Next thing I knew, he was a big baseball superstar, and the thing that happened started to feel to me like it had been a lot bigger to me than it was to him.

And now he was engaged to Lauren Applegate, the gorgeous dancer turned fashion blogger who, by the looks of her Instagram account, was amazing.

"We can do this, team!" Kit said as she pushed the sliding glass doors that led out to the deck all the way open, giving that indoor/outdoor feel.

"It looks so pretty." My voice was wistful as I took in the country-chic place settings on the table on the deck. The white lights in the trees. The peony bouquets. The clothesline filled with photos of Lauren and Ian.

"You think?" Kit had a wild look in her eye. She fiddled with the docked iPad and started to play *Eye of the Tiger.*

So that's where I get it.

"It's amazing." I looked more closely at the photos as Lizette rearranged them for the umpteenth time.

There they were at Safeco Field, Ian in his Mariners uniform. And there they were at Coors Field, Ian in his Rockies uniform, post-trade. A road trip in Ian's truck. A hike somewhere in Denver. All smiles, with friends roasting marshmallows. Bundled up throwing snowballs. Kissing by the ocean, with a soft glow on their faces.

They looked happy.

"Hello?" The sound of the front door opening followed by Ian's almost but not quite familiar voice made me flutter inside a little.

"Game time." Kit squared her shoulders and cracked her knuckles as she made her way from the kitchen to the entryway.

"I'm excited to meet this girl," Lizette said. "I've never met a dancer turned logger."

"Or . . ." I said. "A dancer turned lifestyle blogger."

"What?"

The quiet that had settled on the B&B mid-morning was replaced with the sound of friends and family.

The guests included Ian; Lauren; Lauren's sister Brooklyn; Ian's friend from college, James; Lauren's friends, Cassie and Amanda; and Lauren's mom, Kelly. Sadly, Lauren's dad, Earl, passed away when Lauren was nineteen. Kit, who knows that loss all too well, took special care to include photos of him and even cooked deviled eggs, which Lauren jokes is the only food he knew how to make.

And since Ian's parents were in Ireland, where the wedding was going to be held, Kit had made sure to include some Celtic designs too.

"Kit and Gabby! I recognize you guys from pictures on the B&B website!" Lauren greeted us with a bright white smile. Then she handed us each a pretty Body Shop gift set. "Thank you for having us!"

"It's our pleasure at The Barn Quilt B&B to serve you and all of your needs," Kit said in a weird professional voice that sounded like she was reading from the website. "We take pride in our family farm tradition. From our barn to our beds to our famous Big Breakfast."

Wait. That was verbatim from the website.

"Hey Gabby." Ian leaned in to give me a hug. "Long time no see."

"It's good to see you," I said with a warm smile. And in that moment, it was like something happened in the space-time continuum, and I honestly felt like I had seen him just yesterday. Of course, then I caught Lauren's eye and instantly felt bad for having had a crush on her fiancé ten years ago. "I mean, um, all I see when I look at you is a blob in some clothes, but you know, still, good to see you."

"So this is Gabby?" Lauren's mom Kelly said. "I bet she has some good dirt on our boy."

"No." I shook my head super fast. "I don't have any dirt. Why would I? I don't."

"Come on," Kelly gave me a wink, "you have to tell us something."

"Um." I tried not to look at Lauren, because I was sure she could smell the faint scent of leftover teenage crush. "Aren't you the guy who worked at your uncle's diner and became friends with that really smart girl who lived with her single mother."

"That's *Gilmore Girls*," Lauren's sister said.

"Oh." I frowned. "I thought that was him. Sorry. Anyway. I better go help with stuff." I scurried off and proceeded to water a fake plant.

Ian smiled at Lauren. She smiled back and slipped her hand through his.

Here's what I knew about Lauren: she used to be a dancer and went to Juilliard and danced in companies all across Europe and the US. Now she runs her own dance studio in Denver and has a healthy lifestyle blog. She and

Ian met when he was visiting one of her dance students, who was diagnosed with leukemia, for the Make-A-Wish foundation. She lives in Denver, as does Colorado Rockie Ian. She has very elegant taste. And Kate Middleton hair.

"Shall we proceed to the backyard dining pavilion?" Kit asked in an odd, super professional voice.

Backyard dining pavilion? What? For all the years I've been here, it's just been a regular old deck.

I stood back as everyone "proceeded to the backyard dining pavilion" and took their seats at the places marked by little burlap hearts.

"So you're Gabby." I felt a hand on my back. It felt strangely cold. I turned my head to see Lauren's sister Brooklyn. She seemed a lot older than Lauren. And there was something about her that immediately intimidated me.

"*This* Gabby?" Brooklyn held her phone in front of my face.

My throat tightened. Because there, on her phone, was a photo of me and Ian. It had been taken at a party Ian had taken me to after his graduation. And then, like a year ago, somehow some magazine got a hold of it and it started showing up online everywhere with crazy headlines.

Ian O'Connell Falls for High School Sweetheart! Ian O'Connell Off the Market!

"That is me," I said. "But all that stuff is made up."

"So you never dated Ian?"

"No."

"And you never wanted to?"

"Trust me," I said. "Ian and I were never more than friends."

"You didn't answer my question." Brooklyn smiled and waved at Lauren, who was clearly looking to see where her big sis was. "Look. I made a promise to my dad that I would make sure nothing ever hurts her. And I am going to keep it."

"Well you have nothing to worry about with me," I said.

Then, just to have something to do other than stand there, I picked up the big, fake potted plant I had pretended to water earlier and walked onto the *pavilion*, plant in my arms. As a few heads turned at the sound of my shoes on the decking, I awkwardly set the plant down next to the table and added a super weird Price is Right-esque hand motion.

"To add to the ambience," I said.

"Thank you, Gabby," Aunt Kit said. "As I was saying, tonight's rustic feast is made from only the freshest of ingredients from our organic garden, prepared with the greatest of care, and, can I just say it, *love*."

"We sincerely hope you enjoy your time at the B&B which is known as . . ." Annie was trying to mimic Kit's hotel commercial voice as she read from a small blue card. ". . . A little bit old lady-ish . . . wait . . . no . . ." She flipped to the next card.

Oh my gosh. She was reading comment cards.

"Off the beaten path and covered in quilts." She nodded and disappeared inside.

Satisfied with her talk with me, Brooklyn took her seat next to her husband and dinner began. We served the salad and soup and the guests talked over the sound of the playlist I'd put together of happy, sweet engagement-y songs.

I leaned against the kitchen counter and watched the happy couple from a slight distance. Ian could not take his eyes off Lauren.

Of course my mind went to Dillon.

He used to look at me like that. Well, sometimes. Like when I cooked him bacon.

Kit came rushing in. "What did she say to you?"

"Who?" Lizette asked, suddenly appearing. I swear that woman has a drama detector.

"The sister."

"Nothing." I waved it off as Cat Sajak made a rare appearance outside the master and weaved his way between my ankles. "But this whole thing is kind of depressing. Happy for them. Sad for me."

"You need to get your mind off all this." Annie grabbed my hand and pulled me into the front den. "Here. Take a seat. You can help me practice for my Guided Hypnotic Practitioner certificate."

"Okay."

"Great!" Annie arranged some 5 x 7 cue cards that were in her pocket. "Okay. First. Close your eyes."

I closed my eyes.

"Now. Imagine you are in a thick, green pustule."

I opened one eye. "Huh?"

"That's not right. Hang on. I need my glasses." Annie ran to grab her purse and returned with her bright purple glasses perched on her nose. "Okay. That's better. Imagine you are in a . . . oh! A *pasture*. You have no worries. Your body is lard. Sorry. You body is *light*. Your mind is light. Your forehead is . . . what? Oh, forget these cards."

Truth? All I really saw when I closed my eyes was my secret wedding Pinterest board. With it's fall foliage.

And vintage place settings. And s'more station. With a Dixieland band that will play and my dad will do his goofy dance moves, while playing his banjo.

"It'll happen sweetie," Annie said. "He's closer than you think."

Whoa.

I felt a tiny smile come to my lips. I hopped off the barstool and kissed Annie on the cheek. "Thanks, Annie."

In a weird way that had worked.

I didn't want to be the sad girl at a beautiful engagement party. This was a happy occasion. And I love being happy for other people.

I was about to ask Kit what she needed help with when she came rushing into the den.

"They want you to do psychic readings!"

"What?"

I focused on Kit who was suddenly right next to me. "I was telling them all the things we offer here at the Barn Quilt B&B. And I just kind of mentioned that you're a psychic reader. And they said they wanted to do readings. They were all super excited about it."

"But . . . Kit! I've only been doing that for a week. And I really, *really* stink at it."

"Gabby." She took me by the shoulders, super intensely. "If you don't do this for me, you will be single-handedly ruining my entire life. I might as well close up the place right now. Because if I can't provide those people with an experience that includes a state of the art psychic reading, then I really have no business being in the hospitality industry." I think she was trying to make herself cry.

"Come on, Gabby!" Annie added. "You can do it!"

"Plus." Now Lizette was in the room. "You really owe your aunt, don't you think? She let you live with her all those summers."

"I know I absolutely owe Kit. I'll scrub toilets. I'll do dishes. Anything but this."

"Is there a problem with the psychic?" Lauren's mom, Kelly, appeared in the wide doorway.

"Not at all!" Everyone froze.

Kit shot me a pleading look.

"Just . . . getting into the right headspace before heading out to do your readings," I said.

Kit squeezed my hand in gratitude.

I released a breath.

"Do you need anything?" Annie asked as she looked into her purse. "I think I have some fortune cookies in here."

"I'm good." I headed for the door.

No big deal. Just like at work.

"Here she is." Kit introduced me with a flourish. "Psychic at one of Seattle's leading psychic networks, and my beautiful niece, Gabby."

"Hello." I did a weird wave. "You guys met me earlier. But what you probably don't know is that I do in fact work as a psychic. And I'm going to do some psychic readings for you." I let out a long breath and noticed Ian looking at me, his head tilted.

"Oh come on," Brooklyn said. "She doesn't look like a psychic."

"A skeptic," I said. "That might interfere with the readings."

"She thinks having a PhD means she can't have fun," Lauren said. "Some of us have open minds."

"Here." Annie pointed to a modern rattan chair. "We saved you a seat."

"Thanks." I sat down. I closed my eyes and tried to think of guy stuff. I took a few deep breaths. Then I slowly opened my eyes. "All right. Let me . . . um . . . read the energy out here to see who I should start with." I closed my eyes. And I sniffed the air. Then I moved my hand in front of my face the way people do when they're trying to smell wine. "I'm getting . . . who is the male who works with children?"

Ian's friend James raised his hand. "Does volunteer soccer coach count?"

"It does!" I motioned for James to come over to the chair that Kit had put in just the right spot.

Time to show my abilities.

"For you, James, I see . . ." I closed my eyes again. "Oh . . . a new vehicle."

"No way." James stared at me. "I've been thinking about buying a new car."

"Awesome," I said. "Let's see what else comes through . . . I see the number five . . . and . . . a walrus. Does that mean anything to you?" I asked James.

"My birthday is on the fifth. But a walrus . . . I don't know . . ."

"It may be your spirit animal," I said, trying to keep my soothing tone. "With its tusks and it's . . ." what the heck else does a walrus have? ". . . largeness."

"Okay." James nodded. "Anything about a girl?"

"Well . . ." I looked at the sky and nodded. "Yes . . . absolutely . . . You should go for it. "

James nodded his head.

"Can I go now?" Lauren clutched her half-moon pendant necklace, which was expertly mixed with others in that special way I couldn't pull off. "I mean, if the energy is okay."

"The energy is always okay for the bride-to-be," I said, feeling my face start to blotch. Thank goodness we were in semi-low light.

James vacated the seat for Lauren.

"So, um, first, off the psychic record," I said. "You might notice me getting a little red during these readings. That's just something that happens. Like how that Hollywood Medium kid starts to sweat. So no need to worry."

"Okay." Lauren smiled at me sweetly.

"All right. Now. Back to the psych . . . ia . . . try. Here we go." I let a long breath out of slightly parted lips. "I'm feeling . . . a secret."

It was a no-fail because everyone has secrets.

"You mean, like, someone told me one?"

"Yes . . . and . . . recently . . ."

Lauren leaned in and whispered. "Are you getting a name?"

"A name?" I asked.

"Oh," I said. "Okay. Yes. I see a . . . a name . . . a C name."

"Are you sure?" Lauren looked at me like she wanted me to continue.

Man. This psychic thing was way easier in person.

"Yes. Definitely a C name. C . . ." I closed my eyes and then opened them again. "Maybe . . . Carl?"

"Carl?" Lauren's eyes got wide and her mom and sister gasped.

"No way." Lauren covered her face. "You didn't just say that. Tell me you didn't just say that."

"I didn't say it."

"Except you did," Brooklyn said under her breath.

"Okay so, technically I may have said it, but you're definitely interpreting it wrong."

"How else is there to interpret the name Carl?" Lauren's mom asked.

Aunt Kit shot me a panicked look.

"Don't listen to me!" I said. "I'm a new psychic. I probably meant Carl's Jr. I love that place!"

"I need to get some air!" Lauren shot up from her seat and walked away, looking dazed.

"You're outside, sweetie," one of Lauren's friends said.

"Well then I need less air." She practically ran into the house.

"Lauren!" All of Lauren's girl squad followed after her.

I threw my hands up in horror and looked at Ian. "Who the heck is Carl?"

"I don't think it's Carl," he said, looking like he was going to throw up. "I think it's Jeff Carlyle. A guy she met up with at her high school reunion who admitted he's been in love with her for ten years."

"Oh my gosh!" Now I felt like I was going to throw up. I ran into the house and found Lauren sitting on a couch in the living room, looking dazed.

"Listen," I said to her. "Please come back outside. I swear I'm a terrible psychic. I have no gift whatsoever."

Lauren just shook her head and said the most heart-breaking thing I could imagine. "I wish my daddy was here."

The next hour or so was a mish-mash of misery.

Lauren, her mom, sister, and friends locked themselves in one of the downstairs bedrooms. Ian knocked on the door and begged Lauren to talk to him. Lauren's mom came out and told him Lauren needed some time alone. James tried to offer Ian bro-comfort as Ian paced in the backyard. Then, after what he thought was enough time, Ian tried talking to Lauren again.

And then that cycle repeated about three times.

All the while, Aunt Kit kept saying variations on this refrain: "The psychic is not affiliated with Barn Quilt B&B. Please do not consider this when writing any reviews. The psychic can be reviewed on pyschie.com."

Then suddenly Lizette pulled me, Annie, and Kit into the kitchen pantry.

"She was thinking about calling it off this whole time!" Lizette said.

"What?" Annie and I said in unison.

"I was out by the herb garden, you know, picking some fresh mint for the lemonade." Lizette happens upon all her gossip when she is in the midst of doing something completely selfless. "And they had the window open a little and I could hear what they were saying in there. And I heard Lauren saying that she has never been more confused by a frying pan. And something about how Ian washes his truck with peanut butter."

We all stared at her.

"Okay. Fine. I knew I might get some of it wrong. So I have a recording on my phone."

"Play it!" Annie said, eyes wide.

Scratch. Scratch. Muffled laughter. "This is Lizette Moore-Fiefer." She was whispering. "It is Saturday,

October 8 and I am recording—Ouch. Stinkin. Something bit me."

The first few seconds of the recording were basically inaudible. ". . . don't really . . . I talked to . . ."

But then suddenly it got clear. Really clear.

"So you think you have feelings for Jeff?" Brooklyn was asking.

"Who's Jeff?" Kit asked in a whisper.

"Jeff Carlyle," I answered, my head down.

"*Carl*-lyle. Whoa. You're getting good psychic girl," Annie said as she ate cheddar cheese popcorn she apparently found in the pantry.

"If you're having doubts," Brooklyn continued, "you shouldn't be having an engagement dinner."

"I just thought if I came here and met his friends, saw his town, I might feel different. But I just can't get Jeff out of my mind."

"You have to tell Ian," one of Lauren's friends said.

"I know."

"Poor Ian," I said, my heart hurting for him as the recording got all scratchy again.

And that's when we heard real, live voices outside the door.

"Lauren will talk to you under these twenty conditions," Brooklyn said.

"Of course," Ian answered. "I'll do anything."

And . . . we were trapped.

Annie sprayed some spray cheese into her mouth. "At least we have food."

I googled a test: how to tell if you're psychic. I failed. Miserably.

I tested my abilities out with a deck of cards. I never guessed a single one right.

I wasn't a psychic after working at True Tellings for a week.

I was a girl who somehow brought the truth out.

And I felt terrible about it. I mean, Lauren was the one hiding the big secret, but if it weren't for me, Ian would still be happy right now.

I tried to think of some way to undo it.

Say I accidentally ate the wrong kind of mushrooms earlier that day. Find someone who could lend me a fuzzy brain scan.

Just before midnight there was a knock on the attic room door.

"Yeah?" I rubbed my sleepy eyes.

"It's Ian."

"Um . . ." I looked around and grabbed a quilt to cover my pajama pants and my well-worn Irish-ish t-shirt. "Come in."

He opened the door and walked in slowly.

"Wow." He shoved his hands in his pockets as he looked around. "This room hasn't changed."

I felt instantly cognizant of the Nancy Drew books on the shelves. The umbrella organizer in the corner. My I-tried-really-hard quilts. My Periodic Table of the Elements poster.

"Mind if I sit down?" Ian moved toward the foot of my bed.

"Sure." I held a pillow to my chest.

"You okay?" he asked.

"Are *you* okay?" I asked. "It sounds like things got quiet down there."

"Yeah." Ian pulled something sparkly from his pants pocket. I instantly knew what it was. "Lauren didn't feel like staying after she broke off the engagement."

"What?" My heart sped up in panic. "No! Ian. I need to talk to her. I'm not a real psychic. I don't even think I *believe* in psychics. I just do it for a job. And I've only been doing it for a week. And then tonight, Aunt Kit was all crazy because you guys had your dinner *here*. I don't know half of what I even said. And that stupid name. I have no idea where that name even came from. I can call Lauren. I can even have my *boss* call her if that would help. Better yet, she can just look at my online ratings."

"It wouldn't matter." Ian looked down at the ring. "Apparently she's been wanting to tell me about this guy, and all the doubts she's been having about things, for weeks."

"Ian." My heart was breaking for him. "I'm so . . . I'm sorry."

"Yeah." He stood up and patted the bed. "Just wanted to make sure you were okay. And that you know it wasn't your fault. At all."

It was such an Ian move. "Thanks, Ian."

He nodded and headed for the door.

"Hey Ian?"

"Yeah."

"If she's worth it, keep fighting. If there's anyone who can win a girl's heart, it's you."

My phone buzzed on the dresser, which was just beside the door.

"Could you toss me that?" I held out my hand.

Ian picked up the phone. And before tossing it over, he noticed the midnight reminder on the screen.

I saw it the second it was in my hand: *Dating Experiment Application Deadline*. I'd sent in the application but forgot to delete the reminder.

"Dating Experiment?" Ian asked.

I didn't say anything.

"Sorry. I saw it as I was handing you the phone. Did you hear about that from Doctor—"

"My roommate Paige found it on a flyer at Pacific Credence," I explained, cutting him off. "Because . . . in addition to my job as a *not psychic* telephone psychic, I also do the cliché medical studies, and other studies. Including, possibly, a dating study."

"Good luck," Ian said, the words weighty.

"Thanks."

"I'll see you around, Gabby."

"Wait." I frowned. "You will?"

"Yeah." He nodded. "I'm in town for a while."

"Oh." I blinked a few times. "Well then, see you around."

He forced a smile and reached for the doorknob.

"Hey, Ian."

"Yeah?"

"If you need to talk. . ."

He was silent for what felt like a long time. "I might take you up on that."

Chapter Seven

When I woke up at home Monday morning, it was a totally different experience than I'd had at the B&B.

No soft sheets or the smell of wafting bacon. Just the crummy mattress I bought from a guy on Craigslist who told me about five times that he slept in it with his two puppies, so it was "buyer beware," and this awful pit in my stomach that I had ruined Ian's engagement dinner. Maybe even more.

All I wanted was to go back in time and fix it. Yes, Lizette's sleuthing revealed that Lauren was going to tell Ian her doubts anyway, and Carl really *should not* be interpreted as Carlyle. But still, I felt absolutely terrible.

So, glutton for punishment that I was feeling like, I decided to check the email I used for all my job prospect correspondence.

Dear Saggy, (Yep, it said Saggy)

Thank you for your interest in Eager Education. As stated on the telephone numerous times, by email numerous times, and by text numerous times, it is my suspicion that the "government employment rate researcher" who called asking about any open positions was, in fact, you. As relayed to you on these many occasions, we do not have any open positions. As you continue in your job search, may we suggest you read the e-book How Any Loser Can Become a Winner, *written by our new tennis coach and former gambling addict, John Phillips.*

Bruno Vitoli
Founder
Eager Education

Dear Ms. Malone,

Thank you for applying at Little Pips Preschool. Unfortunately, as I told you in our interview, you look a lot like my boyfriend's ex. I just don't want the children to be around those bad vibes. If you ever change your looks dramatically, please feel free to apply again. (Just send a photo first.)

Thank You,
Penelope Weissman
Little Pips Preschool

Dear Gabby,

Thank you for your interest in being part of the rad team here at Forever 21. Your application, like, totally, stood out. But you're not quite what we're looking for. Sorry. Good luck!

XOXO
Cassie Fox
Manager
Forever XXI

I fell backward onto my bed.

There it was, right in front of me, proof that I'd probably never teach again.

I was even starting to get a little rusty. The other day it took me a whole minute to remember the Periodic Table symbol for Iron. And I don't think I could operate an eyewash station if I had to.

I honestly had applied to all the private school jobs I could find.

Then I moved on to the public school jobs.

And the tutoring center jobs.

And the Craigslist tutoring jobs.

Now I was seriously considering standing in line for tickets to a Mariners game for a lady I found on TaskRabbit who said she'd pay $50 for someone to do just that.

I willed myself up to get ready for the day. I didn't have to go in to work until three, so I moved slowly and pitifully. I took a shower. I pulled on a pair of jeans Iris had brought home for me from the "over thirty days lost" box in her office a couple weeks ago. (She made me shine her sword and dagger collection in exchange.) I slipped on my favorite polka dot sweater. Even the polka dots didn't make me feel better.

And then came the real kicker.

I grabbed my phone and as soon as I saw my alerts, I felt my chest tighten. Because after sending a head aching, heart breaking message (including *many* online reviews of my *one week* career as a psychic) Lauren blocked me from everything: phone, Facebook, and Twitter, etc.

And then a thought struck me: now was a great time for a Good Little Anything.

I padded into the kitchen and stood on my toes to reach Paige's pancake mix in the cabinet.

"What are you doing?" Iris was sitting on the couch, playing the same exact video game she'd been playing when I'd gone to sleep last night after getting home from my weekend in Cle Elum.

"Making breakfast."

"Why?"

"Just to be nice."

"Get away from me!" she yelled at the game.

As the smell of pancakes filled the apartment, Paige emerged from the bathroom we share, dressed in a pair of butterfly-decorated scrubs, her shiny hair blown dry and put into a high ponytail. "What smells so good?"

"Pancakes." I poured a few blobs into the griddle pan. "I hope you don't mind, I used your pancake mix, and your eggs, and your—"

"Hey," Paige said with the swish of her hand. "If I'm eating it, I'm good with it."

"Dang it, Paige," Iris said. "You could have made her wash my car."

Iris, as you can see, loves to exploit our roommate bartering system.

I finished up the pancakes, Paige put out some strawberries, and we all sat down for breakfast.

I filled them in on my crazy weekend, and they, as good friends can, made me feel a bit better.

I was typing "Cooked Breakfast for Roommates," into a note on my phone when I got an alert of a new email.

My insides swelled with hope.

Maybe it was that guy Ryan who was opening a tutoring center not too far from the apartment; he wasn't taking applications yet, but I had sent him a friendly email.

But it was from the study.

Dear Ms. Malone,

Thank you for submitting your application! We believe you may be one of the twenty-five women who are perfect for our study. We're so confident we've even started your profile for you. If you wish to take the final step in the application process, please download the Five Fridays app via the link at the end of this email, and create your private dater profile. (Note: This information is completely confidential and will only be seen by those who are overseeing the study.) If you are chosen to participate, you will be notified by 7 p.m. this Thursday. And as always, as a thank you for helping us with this study, you will receive a $100 gift card for creating your private dating profile!

Thank you,
Dr. Chan, Dr. Whitmore, and Assistants

I read on and found my login information:

UN: GabbyMalone
PW: DATER410

Wait.

Dater 410?

My heart started beating a little faster.

All this time I was sitting around thinking that the study was mine for the taking. That if I decided to do this thing, I could do this thing. I don't know why it never occurred to me that I might be dater 410. And who knew where the numbers stopped. Maybe there was a dater 810? A dater 1210?

I quickly downloaded the app and signed in. Sure enough, there was my profile. Along with a place for a picture.

Welcome to your Five Fridays Dating Profile! Please answer the questions below so we can get to know you better!

What three social media platforms do you most use? Facebook, Instagram, Twitter

On these networks, please provide one to three names that best fit the following:

1. **Old Friend(s):** Ian O'Connell
2. **New Friend(s):** Grady Wright, Roarke Early
3. **Dated Casually:** Jaxon Notting, Paul Minder
4. **Dated Seriously:** Dillon Maxwell

Ouch. Just typing Dillon's name hurt still.

5. **The one that got away:** Ian O'Connell.

Man. That hurt too. But for a totally different reason.

6. What is your idea of a dream date (up to five)?
1. Play Truth or Dare
2. Paper airplane competition
3. Great Date Bag: write down date ideas from the silly to the romantic to the (slightly) scary, put them in a bag, and see where the night takes you
4. Visit a used bookstore and look for hidden treasures

Who are your celebrity crushes (past or present, up to five)?
1. Kermit the Frog (my first crush)
2. Clark Kent
3. The Trivago guy

What things do you wish you could tell your younger dating self?

1. Everything is better with a bag of peppermint salt-water taffy.
2. Just be you! Wear the floral skirt with the Bob Dylan t-shirt and the yellow sunglasses.
3. You will meet a summer boy. You will fall for him—hard. And it will be so worth it. Oh, and so will stealing that plaid shirt out of his truck.
4. Believe that the right guy will come at the right time.

5. And as you wait for the right guy, focus on being the right girl. Do it all! Ask your dad to teach you guitar and practice (the finger pain does go away). Watch as many Christmas movies as you want to! Start knitting—you have an odd knack for it. Perfect your Denver omelet. Add to your umbrella collection.

What qualities do you value in a romantic interest (up to five)?

1. A kind heart
2. Likes to have fun and isn't afraid at all to be silly
3. Has faith
4. Gives me butterflies
5. Makes me want to be better

Next I signed a bunch of forms regarding conduct (basically, all dates should be fit to air on the Disney Channel, which was my speed anyway) and confidentiality (my information would be kept confidential).

Then came a question that kind of surprised me.

Who would you like to invite to join your dating pool? (at least five study-eligible men must agree to join for you to qualify)

___All single, qualifying social contacts
___Only select social contacts (at least seven)

I thought for a minute. If I invited all, it would up my chances. But. No. No way. I'm a fan of all things safe and predictable, like Marie Callendar's pies and Hallmark Channel movies. I made my selection, and after a little bit of thought and reconnaissance I typed the names of the seven guys I wanted to invite. (Here they are in no particular order.)

- Paul Minder (from a double date with Paige a while back)
- Grady Wright (from work, the guy in love with Paige)
- Jaxon Notting (he was pre-Dillon and a pretty cool guy)
- Roarke Early (just another example of what a good coupon can do)
- Andy Liu and Ken Yang (two single members of Ling's band who she said I could include when I texted her)
- Ellis Barnes (a cute guy from Dalton)

When I was finished I clicked *Done*.

And then I saw this question at the bottom: *Would you like to officially join this study?*

Before I could talk myself out of it, I checked *Yes*.

# Chapter Eight

O kay.
Something super weird was going on. I had just gotten home from a post-work interview at a night school, when I checked my email. I had like ten from the Five Fridays study.

New Five Fridays Message:
Three of your invitees have joined your dating pool!
Just two more and you're good to go!

New Five Fridays Message:
Two of your invitees have joined your dating pool!

New Five Fridays Message:
Two of your invitees have joined your dating pool!

New Five Fridays Message:
Four of your invitees have joined your dating pool!

New Five Fridays Message:
Eleven of your dating pool invitees agreed to join the study
by the deadline. Here is a look at just a few of the names.

My heart sped as I stared at them.

Joe T.

Joe T?

Who the heck?

No.

The guy from Big Breakfast. The one who loved his mom a little too much and then followed me on Twitter.

Rob H. As in Rob Hadley, the boy I had a crush on in high school in Modesto, California, who I connected with on our school's Facebook page. I thought he lived in Maryland.

What the heck was going on?

These were NOT the names I selected.

I kept skimming and clicking on the names to connect to where they were on my social media.

Ronald P. That kind of creepy random guy who followed me on Instagram.

Roarke E.

I reached the end of the names the study would let me see and felt my panic spread wide through my body.

Something was wrong.

I shut the phone off and on, but still, the same. (And that one works for a lot of things.)

"Iris!" I yelled. "Can you come out here?"

She came out of her room, dressed as Rey from the new *Star Wars*, one of her many costume choices that I'd seen since the beginning of October. "Yes?"

"Did you hack my dating study account?"

"What? Why would I do that?"

"I don't know." I kept messing with my phone. "A Halloween prank."

"You'll know my Halloween prank if you see it." She didn't laugh. She gave me a death stare.

"Well . . . then . . . can you look at this and tell me what the heck happened? It says all the wrong names!"

"Let me see." Iris grabbed my phone. "It says you sent these guys an invite to the study."

And that's when it hit me.

Tell me I didn't. Tell me I didn't. Tell me I didn't.

"I sent the dating invite to all eligible social media contacts, didn't I?"

Iris handed back the phone. "Yes you did."

Iris retreated back to her room, and I quickly downloaded all my old forms and surveys and questionnaires.

And there it was.

Well, there *they* were.

Two boxes.

I remembered reading them.

__*All single, qualifying social media contacts*
__*Only select social contacts (at least seven)*

Only there, on my form, I had opted to invite all single, qualifying social media contacts.

Even though I could have sworn I checked the other option. I mean, I had typed in seven names. Where did those go?

I buried my face in my hands.

This was a big mistake to make. But, I could see how it happened, I was exhausted that night due to the whole

Carl incident. I was malnourished from living on relish potatoes. And, well, I was *me*.

So.

The invitation to join the Five Fridays dating study had gone out to ALL of my single social media friends who met the criteria to participate.

And worse, somehow, I had marked ALL of them as romantic interests.

And, yes, I thought about just sending out a *Ha, Ha, October Fools!* email to them all. But the Terms and Conditions said that I couldn't correspond with them outside of my message account on the Five Fridays app. And if I did, I would have to repay all monies I'd earned plus the additional $1200 that I would have earned over the course of the study.

But not only were my Visa cards mostly empty, I had big plans for the money yet to come. Getting a flu shot. Buying a pair of nice scissors so I didn't have to keep cutting my hair with the kitchen shears. So, yeah, no— paying the money to get out wasn't an option.

I just had to sit there. And wait. And watch as a load of humiliating "sorry to turn you down" emails poured into my study account.

To: Gabby Malone
From: Dustin King, King's Auto
Hello, Gabby. When I said I would give you a twenty-five-percent discount on your emissions inspection—I wasn't hitting on you. I know that might happen in some of those new romance novels. But not here at King's Auto. Thank you for your business.

To: Gabby Malone
From: Justin Forte
*Gabby. This is awkward. I'm really enjoying the records
you sold me. This dating app looks interesting. But I have a
girlfriend. In Iceland. She's real, I swear.*

The embarrassing emails stacked up.

I don't really remember who you are.
*I thought it was clear I just wanted to interview you for
a job. Please be prepared to write an email to my employer
stipulating that.*
Sorry. This sounds kind of creepy.

A whole lot of them were variations on *Please remove
me from your mailing list* because they thought the invite
was spam.

And then it smacked me like a bucket of cold water.

Dillon.

Oh my gosh: Dillon.

All of the others paled in comparison. I didn't care if
my eye doctor got an invitation to try a new dating app.

But I cared very, VERY much if Dillon did.

An invitation to date me didn't exactly say "I'm doing
great moving on from you."

Why hadn't I deleted him from all my social media?

WHY. WHY. WHY.

# Chapter Nine

"Welcome to the Dating Experiment!"

Yep. Apparently, I, Dater number 410, was what they were looking for.

Now I was sitting in a lecture hall at the small, beautiful Pacific Credence University campus. And every nerdy bit of me loved being in that room. The smell of the industrial carpet cleaner. The squeak of the cushioned seats. The clank of the armrests.

Suddenly the lights went down a bit and a PowerPoint came on. Two teddy bears. A heart. *Aww.* Then, *whoa.* The heart broke into pieces. And one teddy bear started stabbing the other.

"Remind you of anyone?" A tall girl with long red hair that went down to her waist spoke into a tiny microphone clipped to her ruffle top.

A big *yes* sounded in unison in the room and I did a quick scan of the bobbing heads. It was a good cross section of the young Seattle dating scene.

"Well then," the redhead said. "You're in the right place. I'm Jen, one of the research assistants in this study."

The girl to my right leaned over and said. "Tanner, one of the other RAs, is in my stats class and he said this is going to be as big as Tinder."

"Cool." I nodded.

"I am going to get us started," Jen continued. "You all should have been given a free download of the Five Fridays app. This app is the center of all we do. So why don't you all open it up."

I opened the app. There was my profile complete with the photo of me that Paige had added. To the right were five little blue tabs: Dating Pool. Calendar. Messages. Forms. Notes. And at the bottom center was a large Help button.

"All right," Jen said. "The rules of this experiment are pretty simple: go on two dates every weekend for five weeks. One of the dates, the Friday night date, the study chooses who, what, where, and the when, which is always 7 p.m. to 9 p.m. The other, your Saturday night date, you do whatever you usually do for dating (See the Help button for more information regarding what qualifies). And to make it even more fun, while on each date, there will be "twists." These are fun, spontaneous instructions that will be texted to your phones. You'll have up to three on Fridays and up to five on Saturdays."

Jen sat down and a woman with shiny, stick-straight hair that I instantly coveted stood up. "And then we'll all meet back here on November 12 where you'll learn the secrets of the experiment." The woman smiled. "I'm Dr. Cindy Chan, one of the lead investigators. Dr. Brooke

Whitmore will be here for that last meeting. So. Let's do a quick overview of the study."

A slide appeared on the screen and I scribbled the notes down on the notepad I'd brought.

- You will receive your date info at 7 p.m. the night BEFORE the date
- You may be paired with the same person up to two times
- Each date will be in a public place (please read the safety information)
- All Friday Night dates will be from your dating pool
- You must fill out your Friday post-date surveys by midnight on that day
- You must make notes in your Saturday post-date notes by midnight on that day
- Some dates may be being observed

As I read the bullet points, I suddenly started to think more deeply about the study.

Honestly, at first I thought it was just a thing they were doing so they could say their app had "a ninety-nine percent success rate" at helping people find love within "Five Fridays." But now, looking at Professor Chan, I was way more suspicious.

This might be about something serious.

But, rather than get too freaked out, I reminded myself that I've done a lot of experiments both as the studier and the studied. And the best thing to do was just go along as normal. Don't overthink it. Like the time I got a fake side effect booklet when I was in a study for a new cinnamon flavored chewing gum. Suddenly I thought I had "severe tooth shift." Your mind can really play tricks on you.

"All right then," Research Assistant Tanner stood up. "Let's get this thing started with a little Friday night Speed Dating!"

The room filled with whispers and buzzes.

"You'll each have seven two-minute speed dates. You will know your time is up with each dude by this sound." A soft *Ding* sounded from the sound system. "Now go!"

The women stood up and started to move, but everyone looked confused.

"You have all been texted a room number," Jen said with a glare at Tanner. "Find your classroom. Find your seat. And your dates will come to you. Happy Dating!"

Happy Dating. Happy Dating. Happy Dating.

I repeated the words to myself as I maneuvered through the group of women out into the hall. About six minutes later I was in a room with four other women, all of us cordoned off from each other with room dividers. A research assistant I didn't remember seeing in the lecture hall stepped into my mini-room and handed me a folder.

"Thanks," I said.

But he was already on to the next. And he had headphones on.

I flipped through the folder and found pages of suggested "getting to know you" questions. I thought that was pretty smart.

Then, on the last page, were questions about who we liked.

My heart started to move to my throat.

"Here we go." The research assistant opened the door and I could hear the rumbling of men, but because of the way things were set up, I couldn't see them or make out anything they were saying. I took in a huge breath and braced myself.

The first man to walk into my study room was that Jason guy I met at the B&B.

"I'm impressed," he said as he slid into the desk opposite mine. "This is one of the more creative ways a girl has tried to date me." He winked.

"Yep," I said. "That's definitely what's happening here."

"You're looking pretty good tonight," he said.

"Thanks." I think. I looked down at the suggested questions. "So I have these questions here . . . Let's see. Here's a good one. What are you most proud of in your life?"

"*Most* proud of?" He draped a well-muscled arm on the back of the chair.

"That's what it says."

"I dated this girl, for like six months, who looked *exactly* like Olivia Wilde." He reached for his phone. "Wanna see?"

"That's okay." I lowered my head and rolled my eyes. "How about. What would you do if you won the lottery tomorrow?"

"Private jet. Armani suits. Lambo to Vegas!"

O . . . kay . . .

Ding. Time for the next guy.

"Bye, Jason," I said as he stood up.

"Take it easy, Galley."

"It's Gabby," I said as I pointed at the nametag prominently placed on my floral print bowknot dress . A galley is the tiny, smelly, kitchen on a boat.

That's when the next guy appeared.

And a hot wave of humiliation came over me.

It was Paul Minder, this guy who Paige set me up the day after Dillon left for Mexico the first time and told me he thought it would be best if he were "unattached." Paige was dating Paul's best friend Kipson, and the two of them invited the two of us—both recently dumped—to hang.

But while Paul seemed fine, I was not ready for a hang.

At all.

We went to get burgers and I got choked up over everything that reminded me of Dillon, which included a ketchup packet, the smell of onions, and a Taylor Swift song, which I sang aloud to.

"Hey, Gabby." He waved at me like he was afraid of me.

"Paul. How are you?"

"Good. How are *you*?"

"I'm good." I gave him a look that said, I'm sorry about the last time. "You?"

"Actually." He sat down. "It's really nice to see you not holding onto a French fry that you think looks like your ex-boyfriend's left leg."

"Oh my gosh!" I lowered my head in shame. "I forgot about the French fry. So. Clean slate?"

Paul nodded.

"Awesome." I consulted my folder of questions. "Mind if I ask you some stuff about yourself?"

"Not at all." He smiled. And I realized how cute he was. Hazel eyes. Thick brown hair cut just right. Slightly big ears, which I find super adorable. I felt bad for not noticing before.

"Cool." I flipped through the pages. "Oh. Here's a good one. Who was your first crush?"

Paul barely blinked before saying, "Jenna Delafino. In third grade. She was by far the best on the monkey bars. And I was impressed."

I laughed. It felt good. "How did it end?"

"She stole her dad's Rolex and put it in my box on Valentine's Day. My mom found it under my bed, being used as a belt for one of my GI Joes. Then my mom called Jenna's mom and it just wasn't the same between us. After that, Jenna ran away from me on the playground."

"Young love," I said with a dramatic headshake.

"That's right," Paul said with a chuckle. "I have to admit, I was kind of surprised to get your invite to this new app study."

"Yeah." I paused. "It kind of just worked out that way."

Ding.

"That's my cue," Paul said.

And as I smiled and waved, I thought to myself, *Maybe something is working out in my favor.*

Until.

"Hello again, Gabby!"

"Ah!" I jumped at the sight of the guy in the chair across from me.

It was my personal trainer.

Well, more like, my *former* personal trainer.

I booked him back when I found a Groupon for three free sessions at a gym that was closer to Dalton. I liked the idea of a new gym near my new job and I'd been doing my trusty 15/15/15 workout (fifteen minutes on the treadmill, fifteen on the Stairmaster, fifteen on the elliptical) for as long as I could remember—so it seemed time to try something new. I thought it might be the beginning of a beautiful gym-lationship.

But it was not.

Instead, Brock put me through one of the most miserable hours of my life. I lifted things that shouldn't be lifted. I bent in ways that shouldn't be bent. I never went back for my last two sessions.

"All right," he said intensely. "Spill it. Who did you leave me for?"

"What do you mean?"

"Was it Brian Leftwood?" he continued. "Because he comes across all balanced with his yoga and Pilates training, but he wouldn't know how to counteract tight hamstrings if he tried. Or was it that new kid, Andy? He may seem young and fun, but he would only hurt you."

"I didn't leave for anyone." I leaned in. "It just wasn't right for me."

"That's fine." Brock folded his arms across his beefy chest. "I can forgive you for leaving me under one condition."

"Okay . . ."

"Have you met your one month fitness goals?"

"Um . . . I think . . ." I said. "I've been doing Fitness Blender videos on YouTube and—"

"YouTube?" Brock said through gritted teeth. "Now I'm really hurt."

"I'm sorry," I said. "Thanks for coming to this thing tonight."

"I wanted to see you one last time."

"Um." I stared at him for a second. "Is it cool if I ask you one of these getting-to-know-you questions?"

"Sure."

"What would you save if your house were on fire?"

Brock thought for a while. "My whey protein. No wait. My pea protein. No. The whey."

"Cool." I consulted the page again.

Ding.

"I guess this is good-bye," Brock said.

"I guess so," I responded.

"Just don't forget who taught you how to," Brock closed his eyes, "flip a tire."

And then he was gone.

After about a minute had passed, a guy who I didn't recognize poked his head in. "Hi." He squinted, his eyes scanning my nametag. "Are you Gabby?"

"Yeah," I answered. "And you are?"

"Ryan. Ryan Blanding."

That's right! Ryan Blanding. The owner of a new tutoring center. I connected with him on LinkedIn.

"I'm sorry I'm late," he said. "I opened this new business, and I'm trying to make sure we're fully staffed."

Awesome! I celebrated on the inside.

I stood up fast, almost taking the desk with me, and extended my hand as I robotically said, "That is fine, Mr. Ryan Blanding. I understand that life happens."

The creases in his forehead softened. "Thank you. So. What next?"

"Oh." I smiled broadly. "I have some questions here." I ran a finger down them quickly. Then looked up and locked eyes with him. "That's right man, I read fast."

"Okay . . ."

"So tell me, Ryan Blanding," I leaned in.

"You can call me Ryan."

"All right. Ryan. If you could live anywhere—"

Ding.

"Sorry." He grimaced at me as he stood up. He seemed like a nice guy. "That's my fault for being late. But it was nice meeting you, Gabby."

"Gabrielle Malone," I said, shouting out my resume header as he left. "1367 Wall Street #412, Seattle, Washington! My personal interests are thrift shopping and learning how to ski."

"Hi, Gabby!" Joe, who I instantly recognized, popped his head in. He was smiling. But he was all darty-eyed. Then, after a second, he poked his head back out and I heard him say, "Okay Mom. The coast is clear."

"*Mom?*" I said aloud.

"Hello!" A woman with greying curls and the look of a woman who works at See's Candies took me into a huge hug. "I'm so happy to meet you, Gabby!"

"Hi!" was all I could manage.

"So." The woman looked at me as she sat down in the chair, leaving Joe standing behind. "I'm Loretta."

"Nice to meet you."

"Your skin seems rather pale, dear," Loretta said. "You're not one of those vegans are you?"

"Nope."

"Good," Loretta said with a wave. "God did not create Italian food for us to go and make it without cheese."

"Well I eat cheese," I said.

"That's wonderful, dear." She regarded my folder. "What's that?"

"It's a list of questions. Stuff to help me get to know Joe better."

"Well, ask away," Loretta said. "We only have a couple minutes."

"Let's do it." I moved my hands down the list. "Here's a cool one. If someone made a movie of your life what star would you like to play you?"

"Um . . ." Joe tilted his head.

"George Clooney!" Loretta said quickly. "*ER* era George Clooney. Ever since Joey was a kid people have been telling me he looks *exactly* like George Clooney."

"Really? I was getting more of a George Jetson vibe."

"Plus," Loretta continued. "George waited a long time before he found his true soul mate. He was fine not being married and taking his mom to his events. For years."

"I think I remember that." I looked back at the questions.

Loretta reached for the paper. "Let me see that, dear. Oh! Here's a great one. Who is your best friend and why, Joey?"

She folded her arms and looked over at Joe.

"It's you, Ma," he said. "Hands down."

"That's sweet," I said. "Do you have other friends that you work with, or went to school with?"

"He's not done with the last question." Loretta shot me a disapproving look. "Who is your best friend and *why?*"

"Oh." Joe looked at me. "My mom is amazing. She taught me everything I know."

"He was potty trained at two," Loretta added with a nod at me.

"Way to go, Joe," I said awkwardly.

"So." Loretta surveyed me. "Do you mind if I ask you a few questions?"

"Okay."

"Do you wash and iron? Or do you *dry clean?*" She said dry clean like she was saying something really terrible. Like, "throw things at young children."

"Wash and, if I really have to, iron."

"I could probably work with that," Loretta said.

Ding.

"Is time up already?" Loretta asked.

"Two minutes never seems like two minutes." Joe held out his arm for her to take.

I waved good-bye to them both and thought, *So this is dating.* Maybe I was smart all these years to be spending Saturday nights knitting and watching Discovery Channel.

The next guy walked in.

I instantly recognized him. It was motorcycle riding, dangerously charming Roarke, the last of the guys from the little B&B set up.

I couldn't help but think, *Aha!* So the study was putting me with the guys I met most recently. That had to mean something. But what?

But what?

Roarke smiled his "I'm Trouble" smile. "So you want to date me."

"Yeah," I said, attempting a flirty tone. "I'll date you like I'm carbon dating."

He lazed into the seat then leaned in across his desk. "This thing pays $100 an hour. Plus free food and other dating necessities."

"That it does."

"Thank you for inviting me on. I'm sure you have guys lined up for you."

He just couldn't help himself.

"So," Roarke said. "I have an idea."

"Oh, yeah?"

"Yeah."

"We both say yes to this thing, and we go out and live it up at a crazy restaurant or wherever they send us."

"I don't know if this is allowed," I said, ducking my head. "You telling me to pick you."

"Just sharing an idea." Roarke leaned back in his chair.

It was so clear that in school he was the guy in the back of class. Whereas I was the nerd in front asking the teacher for a pop quiz while harboring a secret crush on the boy in the back of the class.

"So did you have your audition?" I asked.

He nodded, a cat who got the canary smile on his face.

"How did it go?"

"I got a call back," he said. "They're mailing me part of the script and everything! Plus, I got a TV-series audition."

"No way!" I held my hand up for a high five. When his palm hit mine, I felt something. "So. Anyway. While you're here. Let's see what I'm going to ask you." I scanned the questions. "Oh. Here we go. A classic. What would you take to a deserted island with you?"

"How many things are we talking?" he asked.

"I don't know . . . five."

"A tarp. A fishing pole. A machete. A photo of my family. And a working satellite phone."

"Ha, ha."

"Let me ask you something," he said, grabbing the list playfully, without permission. "What time in history would you like to have been born?"

"The fifties," I said without a thought.

"Tell me more."

"The fifties were made for girls like me. The clothes. The music. The milkshakes."

Roarke nodded.

"Now let me ask you one." I reclaimed the list. "Ah. What's the most adventurous thing you've ever done?"

Roarke thought for a moment. "Australia."

"Tell me more," I said, repeating his own words.

"I bought a plane ticket to Australia, packed, and went. No hotel reservations. No plan. Just made it up as I went along."

"I could never do that," I said.

"Sure you could."

Ding.

Roarke looked over his shoulder then slowly stood up. "I'll see you, Gabby. You know. If I make the cut."

I let out a breath as he left.

Then I sat and waited for my next speed date.

A couple minutes had passed when Jen poked her head in. "Hi, Gabby. You can go ahead and fill out the form in the back of your folder. Your last speed date had to cancel because of a medical emergency." She frowned. "He's either a doctor or he's at the doctor, I couldn't really make out what he was saying. Anyway! We'll figure out how to deal with him not being here. So. He may end up being one of your dates after all. See you!"

"Wait!" I called after her. But she didn't come back.

And I just sat there, staring down at the last page in the folder.

Please honestly and truthfully rate the first impression each date made on you during your speed date using this scale: Failed. Passed. Soared.

If I had any intention of guarding my heart and selecting the worst candidates, it went out the window when I saw honestly AND truthfully.

Darn my devotion to the scientific method.

Date 1: FAILED!!!
Date 2: Passed.
Date 3: Failed.
Date 4: Soared.
Date 5: Passed.
Date 6: Soared.
    Dangerously well
Date 7: ??? Didn't get to meet him due to a medical emergency.

Wait.

My stomach lurched, full-on rollercoaster style, as I remembered Jen's words. He is *at* the doctor or he *is* a doctor.

Dillon was a doctor. Whose little patients often needed him outside of office hours.

No. There was no way. He would never agree to this. It just wasn't possible. For a lot of reasons.

Not the least of them being that even if the accidental invite had made it to one of Dillon's inboxes, that didn't mean he'd read it. When we were dating, he had thousands of unread emails every day. And even if he *had* seen the invite, he'd just feel sorry for me for a minute, then get back to making out with his new girl.

And plus, I know plenty of doctors.

And *tons* of people who need doctors.

It wasn't Dillon.

I was fine.

Chapter Ten

I lied.

I wasn't fine.

All afternoon, as I sat in my cube at Totally True Tellings, fielding "Free One-Minute Spirit Animal" calls after Capri ran an online ad, I kept looking at the clock, freaking out as it got closer to 7 p.m.

And when I wasn't telling people why they were a tortoise or a hare, I was crafting a *Why Dillon Maxwell Should Not Be in My Dating Pool* list.

I'd started it at 5-ish in the morning, when I woke up in a panic because I had a dream that the guy who had to cancel our speed date was, in fact, a doctor: *ER* era George Clooney. But then suddenly *ER* era George Clooney's face morphed into Dillon's, and Dillon told me he had signed up for the study because he thought it was fate, and he wanted to give us another chance.

Then, instead of telling myself the dream was silly and going back to sleep, I continued to panic. Because, problem was, the dream could actually happen. Not the George Clooney morphing into Dillon part. But the rest, yeah.

And the freak out continued as I realized, sure, he wasn't great at checking his email, but I hadn't thought of Messenger on Facebook. Or DM on Twitter. It was possible he'd gotten the invite on one of those.

So, I went on the defensive and authored a little message to the research team that I could use if need be.

Reasons Dillon Maxwell Should Not be in My Dating Pool:

1. *I have a cousin who has very similarly colored hair to Dillon's, so it's highly likely that Dillon and I are related. I'm thinking first cousins at least. He might even be my brother.*
2. *One time, when we visited Michigan, he found out it's illegal to hang things from your rearview mirror there, but only AFTER he had been driving with his fuzzy dice up for who knows how long. Which I'm pretty sure makes him a convicted felon.*
3. *He's a doctor. So he took the Hippocratic oath. Meaning he morally cannot do anything to hurt me. And signing up for this study would hurt me. And I don't think the medical board would turn a blind eye. And I really don't want to see Dillon having to practice pediatrics out of a little office back by the luggage in Sears.*

The one reason I *didn't* include: because my heart is starting to heal. And if Dillon said yes to me, and we went out, no matter what the outcome was, it would tear open my only just barely beating again heart.

Oh man.

I needed a distraction.

I clicked onto Lennox's blog.

Hey friends!

Happy Thursday! So . . . it's less than two weeks 'til Halloween!!! I'm slightly obsessed with this holiday. The dressing up. The walking through the neighborhood and getting candy for doing absolutely nothing but being short and cute. This year I'll probably be hanging out here at the hospital, but hey, we're still going to crush it. But . . . I'm not sure what costume to wear and I'm hoping you can help. These are the top three contenders: A flapper (inspired by The Great Gatsby, *of course) Harley Quinn (of* Suicide Squad *fame). Or Alice from* Alice's Adventures in Wonderland. *So many choices . . . so little time . . . leave me a comment and tell me what you'd like to see.*

And while you're at it, take my Halloween Challenge: On Halloween—or any day before Halloween—make your GLA vids, pics, snaps, etc. in your costume. Pretty simple. Yet oh so cool!!

Let's do the Monster Mash!
Lennox

P.S. Check out the awesomeness that these good gals, The Pine Needlers, *are doing in Cle Elum, Washington. They sure inspire me!*

I clicked on the link and found our Facebook page, complete with awesome pictures of our progress, and our Quilting for a Cause goal: 384—which was illustrated by a thimble that was being colored in to show how close we are to the goal. There were thirty-six GLAs in the thimble. Thirty-six! After less than a week!

I couldn't help but quickly read some of the GLAs.

- *Me and my best friends wrote nice comments on our favorite blogs*
- *My sister made "fun activity" bags for my kids (her nieces and nephews) before we took a road trip to Yellowstone. Thanks sis!*
- *I played with my little sister FOREVERRRR*
- *We made hygiene kits with my church's women's organization to send to the areas affected by the hurricane*

There was a photo of women ranging from what looked like 18 to 88 all leaning over a long table covered with the most organized looking hygiene kit station I've ever seen. They were all beaming.

I quickly added my GLAs to the comment thread.

- *I made my roommates breakfast*
- *I saw a teenager, who does not work at the grocery store, put away all the shopping carts he saw outside.*
- *I saw a little girl make funny faces at a baby who was getting fussy as his mom waited in line at the bank*

I looked over at Ling.

Then I texted her, *I think I've told you this before, but your band is awesome!*

She texted back the awe-shucks emoji.

I quickly wrote Good Little Anything on a sticky note and posted it where I'd see it.

That's when my eyes flicked to the clock on my computer: 6:59.

Okay. Here we go.

Ping.

With shaky hands, I opened up the message.

Dear Dater,

Here are your First (but really your Second!) Friday Date details!

Who: Roarke
What: Dinner
Where: The Crab Pot
When: 7–9 p.m.
Twists: 2

Happy Dating!

I never should have mentioned to Paige that Roarke was good-looking, charmingly funny, and rode a motorcycle.

Because now she was convinced he would make a great rebound guy.

My plan had been to go out in my favorite faded jeans and a vintage cable knit sweater. But Paige had insisted that this was not the way to seal cute bad-boy Roarke as my rebound.

So now I was in her room while she quickly helped me get ready for my date. She loaned me one of her favorite date night outfits: a pair of skinny jeans, suede booties, and a really pretty silk blush top to wear under a cool black jacket. She also curled my hair into loose, wish-they-always-looked-like-this waves. And she was doing my makeup like only a girl who does makeup tutorials online could do. I'm telling you, Paige is good at *everything*.

She was in the middle of doing my eyes, when Iris bounded into the room. "Okay. Where's your bag?"

I pointed to the robin's egg blue bag just set apart from the others on Paige's vibrant, eclectic bed spread.

"What are you doing?" I asked, turning my head as Iris started shoving stuff into the bag.

"Don't move!" Paige fanned my eyes with her hand. "The cat eye is still drying."

"Sorry."

Iris stood where I could see her and pulled the items from the handbag one by one. Pepper spray. A Power Bar. Canadian dollars.

"I ran a background check on this Roarke guy," she said. "He came back clean. So I only included the basics."

"Thanks," I said.

"Okay." Paige motioned for me to stand up. "You look gorgeous, Gabby."

I caught a glimpse of myself in the mirror. I had to hand it to Paige. I looked pretty good for a broke, dollar store shampoo-using girl.

I grabbed my phone and checked the time. "Well. Here we go." I gave Paige a hug. "Thank you."

"Of course," she said. "Now go get that rebound!"

I arrived at the restaurant at about ten minutes to seven.

Roarke got there a couple minutes later.

He looked cool-guy good in a grey Henley, worn-in jeans, and his super hot motorcycle jacket.

"Gabby!" He stopped at my side. "So this is going to be fun." He put his hand on my waist and kissed my cheek. Not gonna lie. He smelled amazing. And the kiss was nice. Very nice.

"Have you ever been here before?" I asked Roarke.

"Nope. And the broke actor in me is thrilled at the free meal."

"Good," I said, feeling a little flirty, which is never a good thing for me. "I guess we should—"

I stopped dead.

"What?" Roarke followed my line of sight and his eyes locked on what my eyes had locked on.

Dillon. Dressed in his work clothes. Heading right for us.

And not alone.

Nope. He was with a pretty blonde woman who was dressed in a gauzy floral top and white jeans.

Yep, white jeans.

The uniform of lucky girls.

"Who is that?" Roarke asked.

"My ex-boyfriend," I said quickly. "And a woman who I think is the one he left me for."

"Recent?"

"Very."

I watched like a driver rubbernecking on the highway as the woman kissed Dillon on the cheek before heading away.

Roarke draped an arm around me and said, "Don't worry. I know exactly what to do."

"Run?" I moved like I was going to do just that.

"No, not run." Roarke rolled his shoulders and did that arms crossing move that swimmers do before swimming in the Olympics. "I've been preparing for that part in the TV movie *Perfect Deception*. I'm hoping to get the part of Blaze, the perfect guy with a murderous secret."

"What the heck are you talking about?"

"This is the perfect time for me to try out the material." Roarke draped his strong, tan arm across my shoulders. "I'll just leave out the creepy, I-may-be-a-murderer parts."

"Roarke." I stared at him. "This is a *terrible* time for you to be trying out any material. There could not be a worse time for you try it out. Let's just say Hi and Bye. Quick and easy."

He ignored me. "Maybe I'll try some TV stuff too."

"Gabby!" Dillon appeared in front me. Then he looked from me to Roarke—who still had his arm around my shoulders—and back to me.

"Dillon," I said. "This is—"

"Blaze," Roarke said in a kind of gravelly, almost Batman-y voice. "Blaze Blackwood."

"Getting some dinner before heading home?" I asked Dillon, hoping it would send the message: please head home.

He nodded.

"Awesome." I bobbed my head a few times. "Well. We have a reservation at The Crab Pot. So. It was nice seeing you."

"Why don't you join us?" Roarke asked, his voice telling me he was clearly still in character.

Dillon folded his arms and drummed his left fingers on his right bicep. It was his uncomfortable pose.

"He doesn't want to join us for dinner," I said with a weird laugh.

Ping.

I took at quick peek at my phone.

Twist #1: Over the course of this date, if you happen upon anyone you know, invite them to join you.

My first thought was *What? No way. I can't do that.*

My second: *Hang on. That was* super *specific.*

I scanned the busy seaside and tried to see if I could tell if we were being watched.

Maybe someone was here.

Maybe someone had hacked into the security cameras.

It couldn't be just a coincidence, could it?

I narrowed my eyes at a teen boy who was looking my way only to see he was staring at some cute girls behind me.

"Sorry about that," I said as I clicked off the phone. Then I forced the next words out of my mouth. "Would you like to join us?"

"Well," Dillon began, "That's a hard offer to refuse," he said. "I do love The Crab Pot."

"You can join us if you answer one question," I said.

Dillon cleared his throat.

"Do you have an app on your phone called the Five Fridays app?"

Dillon looked genuinely confused. "No. Why? Should I?"

"Nope." I felt like I could breath again as I moved toward the restaurant. "You can join us if you'd like."

"That would be great, actually."

I forced myself to turn off any feeling toward Dillon— good, bad, or in-between—as we were seated, selected our soft drinks, and gave the waiter our orders.

"So what do you do, Blaze?" Dillon asked, jumping right in.

"For now," Roarke said, "I'm working as a firefighter."

Blaze the firefighter. Who wrote this movie he was starring in? A ten-year-old?

"So how did you two meet then?" Dillon asked, not one to relent.

"Actually," Roarke quickly said. "I'm up here for a bit of a vacation and we met at her aunt's B&B over the weekend. And I asked her out."

Wow! That was the perfect answer! It seemed so real.

Oh wait. It was.

"So you're just in town for a while," Dillon said.

"Who knows" Roarke said, "This time I might just stay." He looked at me.

"What draws you to Seattle?" Dillon asked.

"It's just so idyllic. Every year, I pack up my dog, Toffee, and we head out to my cabin, up in the mountains, and I take time to relax." Roarke was silent for a moment. "Sometimes I paint. Sometimes I write poetry." He put his hand in front of his mouth. "Sometimes I bury the bodies."

"What?" Dillon and I said in unison.

"Pass the butter," he said. "So what about you, Dillon? What do you do?"

"I'm a physician."

"A fellow doctor," Roarke said with an approving nod.

"Oh." Dillon looked a tad suspicious. "You're a doctor?"

"Chiropractor."

Dillon clenched his jaw the way he does when he's not comfortable. And I hid my mouth behind my bread so as not to show my smile.

Because confession: I'd just texted Roarke a list of a few things Dillon dislikes. (Hopefully he did better with my list than he had with Lizette's.)

Dillon is not a fan of:
Chiropractors
Hip-hop Music
Long names (for movies, bands, etc.)

"I just really believe the body has so much power to heal itself." Roarke stared into the distance all intently. "Four years of medical school does not a doctor make."

"That's exactly what it does," Dillon said.

"Well. I'm just happy to do something that affords me the opportunity to travel," Roarke's voice was different, as if he were a new character. "In fact, I just got back from a surfing trip to Thailand."

"I've always wanted to go to Thailand," I said, feeling like the whole thing was real. Maybe I could be an actress!

"It's beautiful." Roarke looked deeply into my eyes. "Like you. I used to go surf down there when I was in college. Until . . . the accident." He got weirdly silent.

"What accident?" I asked, brow furrowing.

"I saved a woman from a shark attack. But in the process . . . I lost my . . ." He looked up wistfully. ". . . favorite sunglasses."

"Huh," was all Dillon said.

"But that's just the beginning of the story," Roarke continued. "Because it turned out, the woman I saved was an undercover CIA agent. And the shark had been genetically modified to attack her. So when I saved her, I had to go undercover too. As . . . a merman."

Okay, yeah. This was definitely the TV show. Probably for the CW from the sound of it.

"Soon I was hiding some secrets of my own." He lowered his head and whispered, "secrets that were tearing me apart, from fin to fin."

"Your meal." Our waiter appeared at exactly the right time.

"Wow, Blaze." Dillon cut into his steak. "Your stories are almost . . . unbelievable."

"I've lived a crazy life," Roarke said, looking down at his phone. "But really I'm just a kid who used to be in a hip-hop group named Everything in Life is Something that You Really Don't Need Until You Realize You Do." He clicked his phone off and cracked open a couple crab legs.

Well played, Roarke.

"A hip-hop group," Dillon said. "Would I have heard any of your stuff?"

"You might have heard our biggest hit on YouTube. It's called "The Song, Song, Song, Song, Song—"

"Wow—" Dillon attempted.

"—that We Sing, Sing, Sing, Sing, Sing," Roarke finished.

"It doesn't sound familiar," Dillon said, looking at me to see if I'd let on that this was all a big lie. But I held my face still and serious. I'm telling you, acting may be my ticket!

"Yeah," Roarke said. "We mostly just played at fairs and stuff in our home state."

"Where's your home state?" Dillon asked as he took a sip of his water.

"Um." Roarke squinted like he was trying to remember a line. "Michigan? No wait. Minnesota? Maine? It's one of the M states."

"You don't know what state you're from?"

"It's probably hard for him to remember things after his traumatic incident with the shark." I put my hand on Roarke's arm.

That's when the waiter came to our table and asked if we wanted dessert.

"Um." I looked at Roarke. And then my phone pinged.

Twist #2: Get dessert. Wherever you want. With whoever you want.

So, after I asked the waiter to box my abundant leftovers, I said goodbye to the guys and drove up to Hot Cakes and got myself a caramel-y molten lava cake in a jar. And I savored every bite as I filled out my post-date survey.

Q: How would you rate the chemistry on this date on this scale: Flare, Flashlight, Fireworks?

A: Flashlight (a very bright one)

Q: Would you like to date this man again? Yes, No, Maybe

A. Maybe

Chapter Eleven

D*ear Gabby of the Future,*

If you ever—and I mean ever—get to hang out again with Ian O'Connell, these are the things you need to remember:

He likes red slushies.
He is almost always dressed in jeans, a white tee, and a flannel shirt.
When his friends are around, he listens to Top Forty music. But he also likes indie bands like Death Cab for Cutie. *And he even admitted he liked that Tom Petty CD you gave him.*
He's allergic to kiwi.
He loves his truck. A lot.
He always notices when you wear vanilla fragrances.
He has the tiniest bit of an Irish accent. And it's basically the cutest thing in the whole universe.
He doesn't understand diet soda.

Two words: Jason Bourne.

I shoved the list back into my journal and ran downstairs to where The Pine Needlers were meeting in the large front room.

I had only dug it out after I got this text early this morning:

So. Gabby. You said if I ever wanted to talk. . . . Are you coming to Cle Elum this weekend? Maybe we could go bowling instead.

Oh boy.

And now I was in Cle Elum, thinking about the Ian list.

This was a bad idea.

"You guys," I looked at The Pine Needlers, who already had eighty-four GLAs on the Facebook page they created. "I'm starting to think this is a very bad idea."

"What?" Annie asked from the couch.

"My not really a date-date with Ian tonight."

"But you like Ian," Lizette said, surveying a sheet of graphing paper, where she was laying out a quilt design.

"Yeah," I said. "What if I end up liking him the way I liked him ten years ago?"

"What if you do?" Kit asked.

"It would be bad."

"Why?"

"Because he was engaged two minutes ago. I mean, I've been dreaming about dating Ian since I was fifteen years old. But my dreams were a lot different than this mess. They definitely had a lot more running through fields of wildflowers."

"Gabby." Lizette walked over and took me by the shoulders. "You know I love you. You know I think the world of you. But you think entirely too much."

"Why does everyone keep saying that?"

"This is what you are going to do tonight," she said. "Are you ready?"

I nodded.

"Go bowling with Ian."

"You guys are no help!" I said as I ran back up the stairs.

A few minutes later, I heard Ian's voice downstairs.

I raced down to greet him. "Ian!"

"Hey-o."

I said good-bye to The Pine Needlers and just as we were heading out to Ian's truck to go to Lucky Lanes, a totally neutral friend zone-y place, my phone made that ping sound.

Twist #1: Whatever plans you had for the night, drop them. Because you are going on one of your five dream dates! The one we've picked: The Great Date Bag.

What?

One of my Dream Dates.

With Ian?

I mean. Sure, as a teenager I wrote a few things in my diary (This is what our dogs will be named, etc.). And drew sketches on graphing paper I found around the B&B and then promptly hid in the bottom drawer of the dresser (This is what our house will look like, etc.). But it had been ten years since we'd had a real conversation before last week.

I really should have seen this coming.

It made perfect "study" sense.

I labeled a guy as a crush. I agreed to go bowling with said crush. It was a great plan because it wasn't date-ish at all. It was just two brokenhearted buds hanging out. And then, bam!

I didn't reveal the news until we were sitting in his truck.

It smelled just like I remembered. A mix of old car smell and the vanilla-scented air freshener hanging from the rearview mirror. "This takes me back." I patted the woven seat.

"It's a great truck." He kissed his hand and tapped the ceiling.

"That reminds me." I pulled a red slushie-scented air freshener from my bag and added it to the vanilla.

"No way!" Ian leaned in to sniff it. "Nice work, Gabs"

"So um," I said, waving my phone in the air. "Now that you're in a good mood. There's been a slight change of plans."

"So?" Ian eyed my phone. "What's the new plan?"

"Well," I said. "That depends."

"On?"

"Do you have a pen and paper?"

"I bet I can find something in here."

Ian fished around in the glove box and handed me an oil change receipt and a Holiday Inn Express pen.

"So." I looked at him. "Just so you know. I'm counting this hang out as a technical 'date' for the Five Fridays dating experiment."

"But it's Saturday."

"Yeah. Well. Every Saturday I'm supposed to date however I would usually date. Which was going to be letting my roommates fix me up or something. But then you texted, and I told the study, and here we are on a technical date. And as such, I have to subject myself to their dating twists, which on Saturdays is up to five."

Ian made his adorable thinking face for a beat. Then he nodded. "I'm in."

I quickly scribbled my top three cheesiest/dreamiest/most romantical date ideas on the back of the receipt.

Buy a bunch of goofy stuff at a vintage shop
Have a progressive dinner
Make S'mores by a campfire

I ripped the receipt into strips and folded them. Then I grabbed the University of Lousiville hat resting on the back of the seat and dropped the slips inside.

"In this hat, The Great Date Hat—" I held out the cap and shook it, "—I have three supremely great date ideas. Things I've always wanted to do, but haven't had the opportunity to. Now." I nodded at Ian. "Pick one."

Ian nodded. Then he stirred the paper slips with his hand. And dumped them all in his lap before quickly unfolding each slip.

"Okay." I gave him a slanted look. "I don't think you got the concept. You were supposed to pick one."

"Why do just one when we can do all three?" Ian raised his eyebrows and put the truck into gear. "I think I can take it from here."

"Really?"

He nodded and pulled out of the driveway.

"Sounds like a plan."

As we drove off, I felt all giddy.

And, just in case some of the geniuses I went to college with perfect time travel in a few years, I closed my eyes. That way this Gabby could go back and tell high school Gabby what was happening.

"Oh. I almost forgot." Ian reached across me and grabbed a light blue plastic bag that was on the floor. "This is for you."

"Ian!" I smiled with joy as I saw the Roslyn Candy Shop logo on the bag. I had a lot of memories of him driving me there more than a few times when I had a hankering for their specialty treats.

He looked pleased. "Glad you like them."

I peeked inside and saw all my favorite vintage candies. I instantly unwrapped a piece of taffy. "Are you kidding? These things got me through my first month as an official west coaster," I said through a mouth of sticky goodness.

"Good." Ian looked over at me. "Let's hope I can keep the trend going."

After a short drive, Ian pulled into the parking lot behind the downtown thrift store. He playfully handed me crazy sweaters and hockey pads before finding me a pair of red plastic heart-shaped sunglasses. And I found him a still-tagged fedora that made him look very Justin Timberlake. Then, in the back, we found an old, pastel bike. Luckily I'd worn a sporty-ish outfit (eyelet top, jeans, and glittery sneakers) because I was planning on bowling, because soon we were riding down First Street. Ian steering the bike, and me balancing on the handlebars.

For our progressive dinner we started with fries at the Sunset café. Then we moved on to tacos and drinks from Don Jaime's. And last but not least, we finished things off with red slushies from the gas station for dessert.

We laughed. We biked. We talked.

And it was amazing.

Like, the best not a date (or date of any other kind) I've ever been on amazing.

Now we were at Speelyi Beach Park next to a campfire Ian managed to make with the camping gear he found in his truck. (We'd driven to the lake after returning the borrowed bike to the thrift store.)

"This is the best not-a-date I've ever been on," I said to him as I slid my freshly roasted marshmallow onto a graham cracker and three squares of milk chocolate. I looked out at the sun as it started to hang lower on the horizon, leaving behind a crisp fall chill, and settled into big blanket Ian had laid out on the sand. He draped a thick black-and-red-checked flannel one around my shoulders.

I pulled it tight around me with one hand. "Thanks."

"This really is pretty great, Gabs." Ian leaned back and rested on his elbows. "It kind of feels like we just hung out yesterday."

"I know." I licked some marshmallow off my hand. "I was thinking the same thing."

"You've always made me . . ." He looked at me as he let his voice trail off. Like he was censoring himself. "You're just . . ."

"Slightly insane?" I asked.

"Not at all what I was thinking." Ian gave me a play-fully stern look. "You know. At first, I wasn't a big fan of Cle Elum. It's a lot different than Chicago. But then I met you, and I really started to like this place."

"Yeah, right."

"I'm serious." He locked eyes with me. "I thought to myself, this is what I've been waiting for all year."

I opened my mouth, but before words could come out, my phone pinged. I slid it from my pocket.

Twist #2: Play Two Truths and One Lie

"What is it?" Ian asked, leaning over to read the screen.

"Two Truths and One Lie," we said in unison.

"Easiest twist ever," Ian said with a fake cocky grin.

"Oh." I lowered my chin and stared at him. "You think you know me that well?"

"I know you down to the Cocoa Puff stuff," Ian said as he sat up straight and brushed some pebbled sand from his elbows.

"A confident man," I said, trying to keep cool while my insides were singing.

"Would you like me to go first?" Ian asked.

"I will." I pulled my knees to my chest. "Okay," I said, taking a second to think. "I've never eaten Swiss chard. I know how to play 'Greensleeves' on the flute, piano, and guitar. And I have never jumped off a diving board in my life."

"'Greensleeves!'" Ian said instantly. "You know how to play it on the *marimba*, piano, and guitar."

"How do you know that?"

Ian tapped his forefinger on his head. "There are more than baseball facts in here, Nancy Drew."

"I'm impressed," I said.

"Nicely played with the other two, though," Ian added. "I know that you accidentally ate Swiss chard once, and never again. And I know that you jumped off

the diving board exactly once, to cross off the require-
ment in swim lessons, or gym class or something, and
never did it again."

"It was swimming lessons. And it was awful." I rested
my chin on my shoulder and stared at the ground while
intermittently catching glimpses of Ian's face. "You, my
friend, have an amazing memory. I don't even remember
telling you most of that stuff."

"Told you." Ian lifted his right shoulder to his ear. And
it was like every move his body made was one hundred
percent masculine. "I've been paying attention to you,
Gabby Malone." The words sent a Aspercreme-like chill
up my arms and across my shoulders.

"Well I know you just as well," I said, shooting Ian a
challenging glare.

Ian narrowed his blue-green eyes, which looked almost
golden in the low hanging sun. "Uh huh."

"Give me your worst," I said.

"All right." Ian stared at the water. "My favorite holiday is Thanksgiving." He paused for a minute and swatted
a bug away from his face. "I found a four-leaf clover in a
field when I was a kid and I still have it. And . . . Hibachi
restaurants kind of freak me out."

I smiled inside. Because I knew which one was the
lie. "Your favorite holiday is Boxing Day, which I'm not
entirely sure I understand."

"'Tis the Irish in me," Ian said with an Irish brogue
that nearly made me want to kiss his Irish mouth.

"I have one more," I heard myself say.

"One more truth or one more lie?" Ian asked.

"Truth." I took in a deep breath as I scooped up a
handful of pebbles and let them fall out through my

fingers. "This is one of the best Saturdays I've had in a very long while."

"Me too," Ian said, his words soft like a breath in the wind.

"But that's not my secret," I said. "My whole secret is this: most of my best growing-up memories have you in them. Jumping into that water with you at the first sign of ninety-degree weather, even though the water didn't seem to know it was summer." I smiled as I looked out at Lake Cle Elum. "Watching baseball on TV with you as you taught me all the rules. You watching me as I played "Landslide" on the guitar." I gave him a little shoulder nudge. "You just might have saved me from a lifetime of writing angry goth music."

Ian nudged me back. "Yeah, well, there's more to my secret too." He took in a breath. "Being here with you, Gabby, with your red sunglasses and your fries for dinner, made me forget everything I wanted to forget and remember everything I wanted to remember."

I felt my lips turn up at Ian's words. Then, we sat silently, looking out at the water, enjoying the light of the setting sun as it streamed out through the tall trees, the quiet peace of the lake. And that's when I felt Ian's hand move towards mine. Closer. Closer. Until our fingertips were just barely touching.

I didn't move a muscle.

Until my phone made a loud chiming sound . . .

I didn't need to look to know what it was. Just that morning, I'd set my phone to go off at 5 p.m. every Saturday to remind me of my GLA goal.

"More secret sharing?" Ian asked.

"No." I sat up, cross-legged. "It's." I quickly typed Lennox's website. "Here."

I scooched over a bit and held up the phone, resting my left side against Ian as we both read the latest post. It felt so good to be next to him like that.

"This is kind of amazing," Ian said.

"I know, right? She's awesome to the hundredth power." Which obviously I, who just said that aloud, am not.

"How did you meet this girl?"

"I've actually only ever met her on the phone," I said. "She called me at Totally True Tellings."

"Interesting," Ian said. "So I have a question then."

"What?"

"Am I allowed to come up with surprise twists to this day too?"

"I guess."

"Awesome." Suddenly, Ian stood up, held out his hands, and pulled me to my feet. "Let's go."

"Go where?"

"Go do something good." He raised his eyebrows.

"Okay." I smiled. A big, wide smile. "Let's."

About two hours later, Ian pulled into a Target parking lot.

"What are we doing here?"

"We can't go empty handed," he said as he unbuckled his seatbelt.

That's when it dawned on me where we were headed, what we were doing.

"No we can't." I winked at him awkwardly. And as we practically jogged through the store aisles, I was grinning the cheesiest, happiest grin I'd grinned in ages.

Three calls to Paige—who wasn't working, but was still a huge help—two texts to Lennox, and about one hour later, a nurse named Anna was sneaking us into room 1204. The room of one Lennox Cade. Ian was carrying a huge gift bag stuffed with bottles of glitter nail polish, an iTunes gift card, a *really* nice pair of headphones, a bunch of cute socks, and enough hair ties and lip balm to last a lifetime. Plus every teen, fashion, and tabloid magazine I could find.

"All right," Nurse Anna cautioned us, "it's technically after visiting hours. So if you hear me say the word Flintstone, that means get the heck out of there. Excuse my language."

We nodded and quickly ducked into Lennox's room.

I instantly tensed up. Not because of the hospital thing. Because of the teenager thing. I don't know why, but teenagers kind of scare me. That's a lie. They really scare me. I'm good around kids. And I'm semi-functioning around adults. But teens? I have this weird thing where I think this is My Chance! and I want to be a super cool twenty-something since I wasn't a super cool anything-teen. But I try way too hard, so it never really works.

"What's up chickie chickie choo choo," I said when we walked in.

Yep. That was the first thing out of my mouth.

Lennox just stared at me.

"I mean, it's me, Gabby," I said. "Aka Misty the Mystical." That one I punctuated with some hand gestures.

"Are you always this weird?" Lennox asked.

"Pretty much," Ian said. I pushed his shoulder.

His eyes flicked to the place I had touched him.

Lennox's eyes doubled in size when it dawned on her who this guy with me was: none other than *the* Ian O'Connell.

Anyone who knows Seattle sports knows Ian O'Connell. He played for the Mariners for two years before making the move to the Rockies. "Dude. You're Ian O'Connell." She looked at me. "You know Ian O'Connell?"

"Of course I do," I said. "He's one of my peeping, um, peepers."

"Some contraband." Ian handed over the Target bag.

"No way." Lennox dug through it like a hungry bear. "Usually I feel weird with the whole getting-free-stuff-simply-because-I'm-in-a-hospital-room charity thing, but Ian O'Connell just handed me a bag of swag. I'm *so* not gonna complain."

"That's right!" I said with a super awkward dance. If you can even call it that. "ROLO!"

Lennox looked at Ian.

"She means well," he said.

"What?" I held up my hands. "That's a thing. I've heard it."

"It's YOLO," Lennox said. "As in, You Only Live Once."

"That's what I said." I could feel the pink heat up my cheeks.

"Here." Lennox pointed at the two chairs next to her bed. "Have a seat, you guys."

"I have a better idea," Ian said. "Let's hit up the game room."

I looked at Ian. Clearly, he'd done this kind of thing in this kind of place before.

Lennox smiled. "I'll text everyone."

"Yeah," I said. "Totes. Coats. Take some notes."

It didn't take long for the game room/lounge to fill with teens.

Ian and I had just sat down on some plastic chairs when a kid, probably around fifteen or sixteen, came inside wearing a Mariners beanie on his bald head. "No way, Paulsen," he said to Lennox. "You weren't punking me. That really is Ian O'Connell. You're really Ian O'Connell!"

"I told you, Connor!" Lennox said.

Ian stood up and gave the boy the sweetest bro-hug ever. "What's up, Connor?"

"How do you know Ian O'Connell?" he said, shaking his head at Lennox.

Soon the game room was brimming with teens and filled with the electric buzz of fun.

"Well, Paulsen," Connor said, adjusting his cap. "Best party ever."

Lennox beamed.

"Hey, Lennox," I called. "Come and sit by me for a sec."

She plopped into the seat next to me.

"I want to know what you think about something," I began.

"Okay."

"I saw your blog post about our quilt group doing GLAs as our Quilting for a Cause project this year. We already have tons of GLAs on that Facebook page you saw. And I was wondering if you had any thoughts about how we could move forward."

"Huh?" her face was blank. Not gonna lie, that blank face made me feel super nostalgic about my teaching days.

"The idea is we are going to do our Good Little Anythings, and we're going to take a photo—or write a note about what we did—and then we'll make a quilt, and each block of the quilt will represent a good deed. And we're planning to auction off the quilts and donate what we raise to the hospital. We're calling them Kindness Quilts."

"I like it." Lennox moved her lips from side to side. "But I have a question."

"Hopefully I have an answer."

"Does it have to be quilts?"

"Well. We are a quilting group. But some of us also knit."

"Yes!" Connor threw his hands in the air as he beat Ian in ping-pong. A few onlookers cheered.

"That's so perfect!" Lennox enthused.

"Why?" I asked. "What are you thinking?"

"Beanies."

"Like knitted caps?"

Lennox nodded and pulled up a Pinterest board on her phone. It was filled with all kinds of awesome hats. "I've been trying to learn how to knit, but it's super hard. I thought it would be a cool thing to do because then I could make hats for my friends who are doing the whole chemo thing. Do you knit?"

"Yeah." My heart started beating faster, like I knew this conversation was leading to something amazing. "I do. In fact, I'm better at knitting than quilting. Way better."

Lennox smiled. "When you think of a children's hospital, you think of little kids. So we get tons of sweet hats with ducks and teddy bears and we get a lot of soft, beautiful baby blankets too. But look at Connor. Look at all of us in here. We're the in-betweens. Too young to be at a normal hospital, too old for a lot of what goes on here. So what if you—"

"Kindness Caps," I said.

And suddenly, everything clicked into place. I knew this was exactly what I needed to do. I could take charge of it myself. Gather my own GLAs. Keep my own record. And yarn was cheap. I knew this thrift store that got the leftover stuff from stores, brand new bundles of yarn, for $1 each. I could make a lot of caps for a lot of kids.

I felt happy, peaceful, and excited for the first time in a long time.

"You know." I hugged my legs to my chest and rested my chin on my left knee. "Lately I've been feeling so . . . I don't know . . . lost. And insanely unlucky. And it really is amazing how a GLA can counteract the sting of life."

"Why do you think I started the whole thing in the first place?" Lennox asked.

"Kindness Caps," I said again to myself.

Oh my gosh! I couldn't wait to get started.

"Can you text me the name of your Pinterest board?" I asked Lennox. "I want to do what is going to be loved by the in-betweeners."

"Done," Lennox said after we exchanged numbers.

"Gabby?"

I looked up and my heart went from total peace to full on freak out.

Because there in front of me was Dillon.

All the kids looked worried. "He told us it was okay."

They pointed to Ian.

"Ian O'Connell?" Dillon said.

Dillon had heard some of my stories about Ian. And he never really seemed to believe my stories about me and Ian and the perfect summer.

Now what's up, Dillon?

"What are you kids doing in here?" Dillon was still standing in front of me and Ian. And he kept straightening his lab coat. Like a bird puffing its chest in front of another bird.

The doctor and the famous baseball player.

I narrowed my eyes at Dillon.

Because this was weird.

I mean, yes, we were in the hospital his patients sometimes ended up at. Yes we were doing something that warranted a call to whoever might be in authority. Yes, this could all be chalked up to happenstance.

But was it?

I looked around the room.

Was someone watching me/us?

Did anyone in here look like anyone I had seen at/near/in the restaurant last night?

Suddenly, my eyes fixed on a kid standing in the corner, on his phone. He looked a whole lot like that kid I remembered seeing outside The Crab Pot. And . . . wait a minute . . . was he recording us on his phone?

Without thinking, I got up and approached him. "What do you think you're doing?"

He held out his phone. "FaceTiming my mom."

I narrowed my eyes and stared at him. "Oh. And is your mom in on it too?"

"In on—"

"Flintstone!" Nurse Anna came rushing into the room. "Flintstone!"

"Um, Anna." I nodded toward Dillon. As if to say, Well, we're already busted.

"What do you kids think you're doing?" She scolded. "Your health is so much more important than a little late night fun! Let's break this up and—"

My phone pinged.

Twist #3: Say three things you like about each other.

My heart sped up.

Even with Dillon lurking near me and Ian, the kids quickly vacating the room, and nurse Anna turning from sweet to scolding, I got a little fluttery at the thought of Ian telling me three things he liked about me.

"I'll text you," Lennox said as she gave me a hug. Ian and I moved toward the door and as we said good-bye, pretty much every kid fist-bumped Ian and thanked him for the selfies.

"Looks like the party's over," I said to Ian, deciding on the spot to avoid all eye contact with Dillon.

"The party has just begun." Ian placed his hand on the small of my back, and out of the corner of my eye I saw Dillon staring.

Ian's hand gently guided me down the hall, into the elevator, and through the parking garage.

Once we were safely in the truck I said, "Oh my goodness! That was amazing!" I took in a breath. "*You* were amazing!"

"Wouldn't have happened without you."

I looked at him, blinking. "So. Um. We got the last twist of the date night."

"And?"

"And I'm supposed to tell you three things I like about you."

Ian grinned as he put his arm behind my head and backed out of the parking spot. "And I'm supposed to tell you three?"

"That's right."

"I'll go first." Ian put the car into drive. "I like that you try so hard. And that you fail, miserably sometimes."

"Hey," I swatted at him.

"It's true." His eyes flicked to me before returning to the road. "But you keep trying. Always."

"I guess that's a compliment."

"The highest," Ian said.

"Well. I like how when you meet people you make them feel at ease. Like, the way you just were with those kids. Amazing."

"Totes, coats, take some notes," Ian said.

"Ha. Ha."

"I like that you're so good to your Aunt Kit."

"She's good to me." I made a pretzel with my legs. "I like that you got all famous, but you didn't change."

"Well," Ian said. "I like that when I'm with you, I don't feel like anything has changed."

"I like that if I went into your closet right now, I'd probably see, oh, at least ten things you've had since high school," I said with a laugh.

"I love that if I went into *your* closet, I'd find upwards of twenty umbrellas."

Love?

These were things we *like* about each other.

Why did he suddenly start saying *love*?

"I love that you hate raw blueberries," I said, easily, naturally, "but you love blueberry pancakes, blueberry muffins, etc."

"It's the texture," Ian said.

"Uh huh."

"I love these adorable freckles." Ian touched my nose gently.

Whoa. My heart went all kinds of crazy. I swear I could feel the electrons in my skin.

And then Ian's phone buzzed from its spot in the cup holder.

"Could you grab that?" he asked me.

"Sure." I picked up the phone. "It's—" The name on the screen hit me like a bucket of cold water to the face. "It's Lauren."

Ian tightened his grip on the steering wheel.

"It just says, 'Call Me.'"

Ian twisted his hands on the wheel. "Two weeks and all she has to say is 'call me'?"

"At least she texted," I said. "That's good."

Well, it was good for him. For me, it was something different altogether. It was something I should have known was coming.

I mean he'd just facilitated the single best not-a-date of my life—including the time I dream-dated Chester Cheetah and instead of giving me flowers he gave me Flamin' Hot Cheetos—so of course Lauren texted at the exact moment I started to get a little dreamy-eyed.

It was not unlike the time I made it all the way to the final round of the fourth-grade spelling bee and I got the word *leprechaun*. And Chrissy Snow got the word *snow*. Her last name! *And* she asked, "Can I have the origin of the word?" before spelling it!

As Ian stared out the window, deep in thought, I typed into my phone:

Lauren Whitmore is one lucky girl.

And I, as previously stated, am not.

When I got home, my Saturday Notes heard all about it.

Chapter Twelve

It had been less than a week since I spent my Saturday with Ian O'Connell.

But it felt like forever.

Especially since I hadn't heard a word from him.

No texts.

No emails.

He wasn't even on social media.

What the heck?

"They're manipulating me." I was sitting on the couch, surrounded by piles of yarn. There were Kindness Caps in all stages of doneness around me. I know I looked like someone who was losing her grip on reality. I felt like one. "They're trying to make me lose it."

"How?" Paige asked from the other end of the couch, where she was watching *Project Runway*.

"I don't know," I said. "They just are." I looked up at the smoke detector. "They probably have this whole place bugged."

Suddenly Iris appeared out of nowhere and sat on the couch next to me. "Trust your gut, Gabby. Don't let them break you." She pulled out a pen light and shined it in my eyes.

"You yourself said it's probably just a silly app study," Paige reminded me. "So they can pad their success rate."

She pulled a brightly colored throw pillow to her chest. Pretty much everything in the apartment's common areas belongs to Paige—stuff from her travels, handmade goods she finds on Etsy. It's the kind of decor I think Jessica Alba would like.

"Don't listen to her." Iris moved her face to within inches of mine. "Don't listen to *any* of them."

Okay . . .

I put on a knit cap, a cute dark blue one that looked like something you'd find in a board-riding shop, and rested my head on the back of the couch.

"Maybe they're disguising it as an app study," I said. "But it's a study about being driven actually crazy over love."

I pulled the knit cap over my face.

"Are they checking you for any of that?" Paige asked.

"What do you mean?"

"Are they having you fill out surveys about your state of mind?"

"No," I said into the cap. "But it's pretty clear that I'm losing it."

"Oh my gosh!" I felt Paige spring up and heard the sound of the DVR being paused. "I totally forgot. I have something that is so going to cheer you up."

"Nothing can cheer me up," I said into the cap. Paige pulled it up and off my head.

And there, in front of me, was a glossy bag of delicious, luxurious beauty product samples.

Fresh. Tarte. Philosophy.

"Told you it would cheer you up."

I kept digging through the bag. "Where did you get these?"

"A guy."

"What guy?"

"An accountant guy. He works for one of those beauty box-of-the-month companies. We went to lunch on Tuesday since my schedule's been so crazy."

"Do you like him?"

"He's cool," Paige said.

That's the thing with Paige. She's fun. And so gorgeous. She has guys lined up for her. But very few of them get past, the "he's a cool guy," stage. But, I'm telling you, when she finds a guy that does, she is loyal to the end. She's still friends with the guy who took her to her sixth grade dance.

"Take whatever you want," she said. "But I'll take the eye cream if there's any."

"Thank you thank you thank you!" I put a few things on the coffee table.

"So," Paige said. "Tell me. Why are you freaking out . . . really?"

I sighed. "Because before I hung out with Ian, doing *the most romantic things I could think of,* he was just this childhood crush who was marrying the perfect girl."

"And now?"

"Now, for the first time in my life, I understand why so many rom-coms in the 90s included the sabotage of a wedding."

"Gabby!"

"I know." I closed my eyes. "I'm terrible. I don't deserve these beauty products. I deserve to keep using the recalled mascara that says, 'warning, do not use near functioning human eyes.'"

Ping.

It had only been two weeks and that sound already haunted me. The other night it went off when I was asleep, and it sounded so much like the kitchen timer that I dreamed I was being chased by the Hamburger Helper hand.

I picked up my phone. Okay. Here we go. I let out a long breath, the way I've seen athletes do to calm their nerves.

Dear Dater,

Here are the details for your Third Friday Date!

Who: Paul
What: ?
Where: ?
When: Friday 7–9 p.m.
Twists: 2

"Good or bad?" Paige asked.

"Kind of in the middle, actually. It's cute Paul."

Except . . . what was up with the What and Where question marks?

Well. I found out. Because Cute Paul remained cute for about twenty-four hours.

Until these date twists came through: your date gets to choose the Where and What of this date. And Paul chose an indoor rock climbing gym. At which point he became Trying to Kill Me Paul.

"You okay?" Paul, who was apparently super into adventure sports, peered at me as I looked up at the people climbing the wall.

How the heck did they get up there by gripping onto those weird little colored things?

"Sure!" It was a lie. I mean, I'm afraid to go up in the Space Needle. "Can't wait."

"So have you been climbing before?" Paul asked. "Or do we need the *lesson?*"

"I'll be fine," I enthused.

I could learn on the spot.

Right?

"Then I think we're good to go." Paul took off his street shoes and slipped into some that looked kind of like a cross between hiking shoes and ballet slippers. Then he stepped into a harness contraption thing and picked up a bag of chalk.

"Oh," he said, noticing me staring at him. "Do you need to *rent* equipment?"

I shrugged as I decided I liked Paul a lot better when we were on my turf. A desk-laden, clean-smelling class-room where people know what the heck the chalk is for!

I shrugged. "I have some, but it's at the, um, rock climbing equipment cleaner place."

"I see." Paul led me to the counter in the middle of the gym.

Byron, the kid manning it, was definitely not old enough to be in charge of this huge death trap.

Byron fitted me with a harness and shoes and offered me some chalk.

"No thanks," I said, too afraid to ask where it went and what it did. "I climb old school."

"Cool." Byron nodded.

Then came the waiver.

Which was all kinds of scary.

And here's the thing. I'm risk averse in every way. And this waiver was making it very clear that I was about to take one heck of a risk.

Paul cleared his throat as he waited for me to read over the insanity agreement.

So I closed my eyes and scribbled different things on each signature line:

I love you, Mom!

I love you, Dad!

Paige, you can have all my shoes!

The sooner I signed, I told myself, the sooner this would be over.

"Well." Paul put a hand to his chin as he surveyed a few of the nearest walls. "I think I'm going to start here,' he said with a gesture to our right.   "I think I'm going to try a four today."

"Cool," I said. "I'll watch you."

"Watch me?" He looked confused as he gathered some ropes and clips and who knows what else. "Aren't you going to belay?"

I was silent for a second. There's a time and place to pretend you know how to do something (like when you write that you're "very proficient" at "Excel" on a job application) but this was a little too life and death for that.

"I think I need a quick lesson."

Paul sighed and had Byron come over and show me how to hold onto the rope so that Paul didn't plummet to his death.

And then he zipped all the way up to the ceiling, only pausing a couple times.

Okay, I thought as I watched him, that doesn't look too bad. I think I could handle that.

"Anchor!" Paul yelled down at me.

"What?"

"Anchor!" he repeated, this time more frantically.

A worker rushed to my side and clipped the end of the rope into a hook on the floor.

Oh.

"Sorry!" I yelled to Paul.

"It's okay!" He called down to me. "I'm coming down."

I held tight to the rope, just as Byron had shown me, as Paul repelled down. He really was cute.

"You ready to go up?"

I nodded and put my hand on the nearest yellow grips, marked with a number one, as in easiest.

Okay. This would be okay. I could do this. Byron showed me how.

I tried not to panic as I pulled myself up, moving my feet from one yellow grip to the next until I was shaking with a mix of trepidation and fatigue.

And then I made a mistake: I looked down.

The people below looked like ants.

"How far up am I?" I asked, my voice shaking.

Byron looked at a height chart on the wall. "Five feet."

Five feet. That was it.

All right. A little bit more. Just to prove you can.

I forced myself up by sheer mental will. But soon, my muscles started to get freaked out.

"Come on," Paul called out, "Don't go all Elvis on me, Gabby."

Elvis? What the heck was he talking about? That's when I looked down at my shaking leg.

Oh. Ha, ha. Good one, rock climbers. Do you not know that Elvis died before his time?

"Okay." I let go of the wall and grabbed my rope. "I'm done."

Paul gave me a hug when I was on solid ground. "I'm pretty sure you just pretended you'd done that before," he said. "Which I find completely adorable."

I breathed in his sporty scent before he let go.

"What do you say we get out of here," he suggested. "There's a frozen yogurt place down the block."

"Now that," I said, "I'm an expert at."

# Chapter Thirteen

Well, I almost plummeted to my death tonight for a guy I'm probably never going to see again!"

I kicked the door closed with my foot and dropped my bag on the floor. That's when I noticed that the den was not occupied by the Pine Needlers—who had been getting together almost every day lately—as I expected, but by a family playing *Sorry!*

The youngest of the board-game-playing family, a cute blond boy with curls, hid behind his mom.

"Um. Sorry folks," I said. "I hope you enjoy your stay at the Barn Quilt B&B, which gets its name from the quilt design that is hand painted onto the red barn." Then I rushed back to find everyone in the back room, which looked like a quilt shop.

Everyone including my mom.

She stood up and gave me a hug. "Sounds like we got into town just in time."

"Where's dad?" I asked. "And the camper?"

"Over at the RV Park," she said.

I hugged her tight, taking in the smell of rosewater soap and fossil fuel. When I let go I plopped down on the couch.

"Tell us all about it," Mom said.

I thought back on the survey I'd filled out at home after I packed my Cle Elum bag.

Q: Rate the ease and comfort you felt on your date using this scale: I wanted the date to end immediately. I wanted the date to end early. I never wanted the date to end.

A: I wanted the date to end early. (He is a good guy. But not mine. Oh, and P.S., we did not get frozen yogurt—we got frozen kefir.)

Q: Would you like to date him again? Yes, no, maybe
A: No.

I quickly dove into some hand stitching while reliving the date. I'd gotten into a nice little routine. I went on my study dates on Friday nights. I drove out to Cle Elum where I quilted and/or knit while the full-fledged Pine Needlers gave me comfort and advice. And then on Saturday, I got to hang out with the only person I've ever known who I feel comfortable with no matter how long it's been since I've seen him.

"Isn't dating supposed to be fun?" Lizette asked. "I mean, I'm always hearing about these new apps, like Timber and Bungle, and they sound pretty fun to me."

"Well I think they sound terrible to me," Mom said, shooting Lizette a look. "Like shooting yourself in the foot with a nail gun, basically."

"Either way," I said, "I'm starting to think this whole dating study thing was a really big mistake."

"Well, why did you join it then?" Lizette asked.

"Because she wanted to," Mom said in a very mama-bear tone.

"It sounded great on paper," I explained. "Testing a dating app and getting paid for it."

"Seems to me you were maybe hoping for more than that," Kit put in.

It was true.

I was looking for love.

"Maybe you need to lower your expectations," Annie offered. "Just enjoy the ride."

I sighed. "Yeah. But I just want to find . . ." I felt an ache in my bones. I've always been not-at-all scientific when it comes to love. A hopeless romantic, if you will. Not so much because of fairy tales or romantic comedies. But because of my mom and dad. Because of Kit and Nelson. Because my whole life I was reminded of how beautiful love stories can be. Real ones.

The kind where a man plays Beatles songs on his guitar while his wife looks at him like she can't believe she got so lucky.

The kind where a woman gets her barn painted, but makes certain the painters don't touch the painted quilt her late husband worked on many years ago.

"I just want to find . . ." I continued. "The kind of love where a girl like me wakes up feeling lucky every single day."

The sound of gentle knocking caused us all to look at the doorway.

And standing there was none other than Ian o'Connell. He looked really good in the soft light of the room, with his clothes hanging off him in that effortless way some guys wear clothes.

It's weird. I know Ian is handsome, but it still kind of shocks me every time I see him after any time apart.

All tan and muscled with his clothes hanging off him in that perfect way some guys wear clothes. Ian was a not-fair kind of good-looking.

I blinked. Had he heard any of that?

"Sorry," he said as he motioned over his shoulder. "The family in the front room told me you were back here."

"Nothing to be sorry for, hon," Kit said. "Come on in and quilt with us."

"Actually." Ian looked at me. "I was hoping to steal Gabby for a minute."

"Ian O'Connell!" my mom said, apparently just recognizing him. "You are a handsome young man! You must be a back sleeper."

I hid my face as I hopped up and moved toward Ian.

"Nice to see you, Jolene," he said. "I was just telling Gabby the other day how she saved my summer when my family first moved here."

"I guess your paths were meant to cross," Mom said.

"I think you're on to something," Ian said with a smile that was authentically charming.

I raised my eyebrows and moved from the warmth of the house to the chill outside, and sat on the deck's top step.

"So what's up?" I said, pulling the sleeves of my knit shirt over my hands. "How did you know I was here?"

Ian unzipped his hoodie and helped me into the large sleeves before sitting next to me. "I've been sworn to secrecy on the second question," he said. "But as for the first, I was wondering if you wanted to go on a not-a-date with me again tomorrow."

"Yes," I said.

And the second the word came out of my mouth I felt . . . afraid.

"Is it cool if we do it in the city?" he asked.

"Sure." My expression turned quizzical. "Why?"

"Because I'm catching the red eye out of SeaTac tomorrow night."

I closed my eyes and took in a breath.

Suddenly I was sixteen again. Sitting in almost this exact same spot as Ian told me he was leaving for Louisville earlier than planned. And realizing that somewhere between playing catch in the early morning light and laying on our backs in his truck bed looking up at the stars, my best friend had become so much more.

"Oh," I said, gripping the wood of the deck.

"Yeah. Lauren and I . . . I just feel like we didn't . . ." He took in a breath, then shook his head. "I need to go to Denver."

"I hope it all works out," I said, genuinely meaning it.

"I know." Ian slipped an arm around me. I forced myself not to think about the way his weight felt against me. Because I couldn't open my heart to someone who couldn't open his back. Even if only for a minute.

"But before I left, I wanted us to have one more Saturday."

"One more Saturday," I said.

And then I forced myself to look up at the stars with my friend.

Chapter Fourteen

Ian didn't even get in a second knock before Paige swung the door open at just a couple minutes past ten on Saturday morning. "Oh my gosh!" I heard her shout. "You really are Ian O'Connell! I spent most of freshman year of college thinking Gabby was lying about being friends with you! Ian O'Connell!"

"Just Ian," I heard him say.

"Hey!" I rushed out of my room. "I just realized I have no idea if I'm dressed properly for today."

Ian surveyed my favorite soft grey sweater, jeans, and bright-striped socks. "You're good. Just grab some boots and a coat. Fall in Seattle is definitely here."

Paige remained in the entryway, smiling as she moved her gaze from Ian to me and back to Ian.

If ever there were a guy who had the Fangirl Effect, it was Ian O'Connell.

"Do I need to bring anything?" I asked.

"Nope." He shook his head. "I've got it covered."

I slipped on my imitation Hunter boots and shoved my keys, wallet, and phone into my hooded jacket. I was pulling my ponytail loose from my coat when my I heard my phone *Ping* in my pocket.

I fished it out and read as we walked down the hall.

Dear Dater,

Happy study halfway point! To thank you for helping us out, we're allowing you to pick your next Friday date yourself. Please make your selection from the following men in your dating pool for your Fourth Friday Date!

And there were four names:

Roarke
Joe
Paul
Ryan

Well. At least I got to pick.

"Hey Ian?" I asked when we reached the elevator.

"Yeah."

"An actor, a mama's boy, a high adventure sporter, or a tutoring center owner?"

"For what?" Ian asked as he pushed the lobby button.

"My next Friday night date."

"Oh. Then definitely a tutoring center owner," he said. "Maybe it will lead to a job interview."

Um. Hello. Genius.

"I knew I kept you around for a reason."

The words made me feel instantly sad. But I shelved them. Right now, this afternoon, I was going to have fun with a guy I could always have fun with.

I made the selection on my phone.

And we were off.

Once we were inside Ian's truck, he turned it on to get the heat started.

"So." Ian rubbed his hands together in front of the heater vents. He was tough and manly and strong. But for as long as I could remember he *hated* having cold hands. Maybe it had something to do with baseball. "Do you remember that day," he said, "I think it was just a few days before I was headed to Louisville, and you told me you'd never played Truth or Dare."

"That's right," I said, pointing a finger at him. "You said you'd play with me some day."

"Yep." Ian peered out the window. "Well, Gabby Malone, today is someday."

"We're playing Truth or Dare?" I said.

"With a bit of a twist." Ian looked out the windshield. "Every dare has to be a Good Little Anything."

"Seriously?" My mouth turned into the biggest, truest smile. "Am I going to be knitting like crazy?"

"Well, since I can't knit . . ." Ian said with a look of defeat.

"This is even better!"

"Well then, Gabby Malone, let's do this!" He shot me a wink. "Truth or Dare?"

"Truth."

Ian tapped his fingers on the wheel. "Do you have any hidden talents?"

"Do I have any . . . Aha! Yes I do, as a matter of fact. I can tell the difference between the colors of M&Ms with my eyes closed."

"You can not!" Ian looked at me like I was uttering complete nonsense.

I crossed my arms. "Try me sometime."

"Oh I will." Ian looked at me with suspicion. Then he reached across the console and clunked the glove compartment open. "Right now," he said as he retrieved a half-eaten bag of peanut M&Ms.

I stared at the bag. "What did you . . . how did you . . . how old are those?"

"A couple days," Ian said. "You're not getting out of this."

"Fine by me."

"I have to keep my eyes on the road," Ian said. "So I'll just have to take your word for it that you're keeping your eyes closed."

"Girl Scouts' honor," I said.

And with my eyes tightly closed, Ian handed over the following colors of M&Ms: blue, blue, red, yellow, brown, yellow, orange.

And I got them all right.

"How the heck did you do that?" Ian looked partly shocked, partly confused, and partly impressed.

"Your turn, Mr. O'Connell," I said. "Truth or Dare?"

"But I still want to know . . . that's just not possible."

I held my hands out as I shrugged my shoulders. "Hidden talent," I said. "So what's it going to be for you?"

"Truth," Ian said.

I watched some people run across a nearby crosswalk. I knew what I wanted to ask. Are you engaged to Lauren?

Is that why you're leaving? But it felt like . . . I don't know . . . I needed to warm up to it for some reason. "Who was your first crush?"

"Marsha Brady," Ian said instantly.

I smiled. "Huh."

"And back to you," Ian said. "What'll it be? Truth? Dare?"

"Where are we going?" I asked as he took us right back in the direction we came from.

"No idea," he answered.

"That's not good." Then I snapped, suddenly struck with a plan. "How about we head to Pike Place Market, do a few random Good Little Dares, and then head somewhere for a big ole dose of, dun, dun, dun, dun: truth."

Ian nodded. "I like how you think, Ms. Malone."

For the next three hours and forty-two minutes we unleashed ourselves on the Market and the surrounding area.

We had some spirit-lifting successes:

We bought Daily Dozen donuts for a big family who were all wearing Tyson Family Reunion shirts, and a bunch of the guys (and a couple of the teen girls) asked for Ian's autograph. We put a five-dollar-bill in the prize slot on a cheap plastic bubble toy machine. We bought a pack of Post-It notes, wrote inspiring quotes on them, and went Post-It crazy. We put flowers and Thank You notes under the windshield wipers of cars with military base stickers in the windshields. Ian helped a mom fold up her stroller and put it away in her car.

We also had our share of fails:

We started out random. I asked a plainclothes cop if he wanted me to give him a free palm reading and he gave me a field sobriety test. Which I almost failed. Ian offered to carry an older woman's fish out of the famous fish market and she started yelling, "Stranger! Stranger!" I asked a woman if we could help walk her dogs, and after considering for a minute, she said, "Sorry. You just don't have an honest face." I offered a kid one dollar to stop hitting his little sister. "No you loser!" He said. "Make it ten and we'll talk."

Then we focused. We decided to wash car windshields. And of the three *I* personally washed, one guy told me he was not paying me for washing his windshield, and I needed to get a real job. One lady ran out of the quick mart where she was shopping yelling at me, "That's not your car! That's not your car!" And one person took a bunch of pictures of me with their phone and said he was going to report my vandalism.

Somehow at the end of it all, we were equal parts exhausted and elated.

Then Ian put his arm around my shoulder. "What do you say we have our final Truth session on Bainbridge. At Mora."

My eyes shot wide open. "Seriously?"

Ian nodded.

And before I could talk myself out of it, I stood on my tiptoes and wrapped my arms around him. "Thank you, Ian!"

He held his cheek against mine. "Thank *you*, Gabby."

I let go and we bounded for the ferry. Ian bought my ticket and let me pick a seat where I could look out the window at the mix of rain and sun that danced on the water.

And then we were there. Bainbridge Island. Truth is, Ian is one of the few people who knows how much I love everything about Bainbridge. It's a little bit like umbrellas to some Seattleites. Mostly it's only interesting to tourists. But I don't care. It's quaint and cozy . . . and it's the home of Mora ice cream.

The best ice cream on the planet.

For real.

And I make this statement somewhat educated. I ate Tillamook when I lived in Portland. Blue Bell when I lived in Dallas. Costco-brand ice cream when I read it won in blind taste tests. But Mora? There's nothing like it.

After disembarking, Ian and I made a beeline for the cute little ice cream shop. And the second we got inside, I relished in the sensory mix of sugar and ice. After a short wait, we ordered our treats. Maraschino Cherries Cream for me and Chocolate Peanut Butter Moreo for Ian.

We took our treats outside and walked a bit away from the shop where we found a wooden planter.

"I have to say," I licked the cold, creamy perfection from my spoon. "Best not-a-date ever."

"Agreed." Ian bit into his Chocolate Peanut Butter Moreo. He pointed his pink spoon at me. "Why do you hold your spoon that way?"

"What?" I held it out, ice cream facing down. "Because I want the yumminess to go right to my tastebuds."

"Yeah, but aren't you worried you'll spill all over?"

"Oh Ian. Let me fill you in on some of the perks of being Gabby. When it comes to food, I do what I want. Because chances are I will spill the punch all over my baby blue eighth grade dance dress. I'll be in the middle of eating a salad made of the listeria-laden spinach at the exact minute Channel 5 is running a story about the recall."

"I learn something new about you every day," Ian. "Which reminds me. It's Truth time."

"You're right." I took a bite and let the treat sit on my tongue for a moment. "What . . . what kind of pajamas do you wear?"

"Do not tell a soul this, but I still wear Mariners pants sometimes," Ian admitted. "How about you?"

"Geeky science shorts and pants with white tank tops. And my Irish-ish tee."

"I can totally envision that." Ian's eyes lingered on me for a moment.

"Um." I cleared my throat. "What's the most awkward moment you've ever had on a date?"

Ian thought for a minute. "I don't know about *most* awkward, but when I was a sophomore in college, I stayed up all night for a midterm, but I still wanted to go to a movie with this girl. I ended up falling asleep on her shoulder and drooling on her. A lot. Turned out it was cashmere, and she sent me the dry cleaning bill."

I laughed and patted him on the back.

"What's your favorite Disney movie?" I asked Ian.

"Uh uh," he said. "Most awkward date moment, please?"

"I've had so many," I said. "But I'd say the one that takes the cake is when I went out in a group with a guy I really liked and the waiter came over and took everyone's order. And then he handed me the kids menu and asked if I wanted some crayons to color with."

Ian shrugged, "Hey, when you're forty and looking twenty, you will love that moment."

I smiled. It was so Ian. He had this way of making me feel like everything about me was not just okay, but good, even great.

"Oh, and," he said. "my favorite Disney movie is *The Rookie.*"

I nodded. "I should have known."

"What's yours?"

"*The Little Mermaid.*"

"I can see that," Ian seemed intrigued as he plunged his spoon into his ice cream cup.

"So, tell me," I said to Ian. "Do *you* have any hidden talents?"

"Hmm." he thought for a second. "I actually learned how to make balloon animals a few years back."

"Let me guess," I said, "you learned before a hospital visit."

Ian nodded.

"Well," I said. "I'll have to tell Lennox about your talent."

"Now that girl is something special." Ian bumped his shoulder against mine. "Not unlike this girl I knew when I was in high school. One who had a had a thing for wearing flowers behind her ear, sundresses with flip flops, and always had Big League Chew bubble gum—which I, eternal baseball fan, thought was *the coolest.*"

"What did you think of me back then?" I asked.

"How long do you have?" he said with a grin.

His words made my ice cream-filled self feel warm.

"Well, that first day I remember thinking there was no such a thing as the Department of New Inns and Laundromats."

I laughed. Hard.

"Yeah. Kit sent me over there to spy. I don't know if I should tell you this, but I'd actually been there, like, five times before you caught me. Checking out the prices. The spa services. The menu. And you. Might as well admit it."

"Well." Ian glanced over at me. "That's another thing I thought. I thought you were super pretty in your yellow dress."

I blinked, and I know I turned red.

"I thought you were smart enough to cure a disease someday," he continued. "I thought you were a really hard worker—pounding nails, pulling weeds, trimming trees. I thought you had crazy taste in music. I thought you ate a lot of potato chips. I thought the water balloon fight we had behind the barn. I thought your knowledge of plant names was impressive. I liked your yellow sundress. And I loved how you always wore your hair up, so I could see these three freckles on your neck." He touched my skin and all of my cells responded.

"Well, I thought you were hilarious," I said without being prompted. "I thought you were so comfortable in your skin, which I envied like crazy. I thought you were kind. To everyone. I thought you were way better at sports than was fair. I thought you were the type of person who could really, truly change the word."

"Gabby?" Ian scooted closer to me.

"Are you and Lauren engaged again?" I asked quickly. "Or, you know, still?"

"No." Ian stared at his cup. "But she did tell me that there's nothing with her and he who shall remain nameless."

"That's good."

Ian's mouth twitched. "I was hoping she could come back here, so we could stay out here until Christmas like we planned, but she doesn't think we'll ever be able to work things out here."

"Why not?"

"Do you really want to know?"

My brow furrowed in concern. "I think."

"Actually." Ian touched the tip of his shoe to mine. "You."

"What?"

"Truth?" Ian said. "You've given me a lot to think about. I think if all this stuff with Lauren had happened a few weeks earlier, if I hadn't done this not dating thing with you, I would have just accepted her apology and she'd be wearing the ring, and we'd still be getting married on New Year's Eve."

"But?"

"But this time, with you, I realized there might be more for me. And that freaked the you know what out of Lauren."

"I'm sorry," I said.

"I hope you're not." Ian brushed his thumb on my chin. "There are people who believe I'm good at baseball, good at keeping up my parents' inn, good at keeping my image squeaky clean while I'm endorsing their products. But you, Gabby Malone, are the only person I've ever met who makes me feel like I want to be, like I can be, just . . . anything"

"Well then that's my last dare," I said. "Do your anything."

Chapter Fifteen

Until next time, Nancy Drew, Ian texted from his gate at the airport late Saturday night.

And I'd spent all of Sunday—with the exception of church—and Monday morning reading it like I thought some secret code was going to jump out at me.

Briiing. Briiing.

I adjusted the cat ears I was wearing on my head. "Thank you for calling Totally True Tellings. Happy Halloween! This is—"

"It's Lennox," the voice on the line said.

"Lennox?" I paused. Then I breathed into the phone like a ghost. "Whoooo!"

"Let me guess," Lennox deadpanned. "That's the ghost of my dead grandmother coming to deliver a message to me on All Hallows' Eve."

"No," I said. "I'm just seeing if my boss is listening in."

"Oh." Lennox got super quiet.

"I think we're good. So. What's up? And why aren't you calling my cell?"

"Well, I feel like I owe you. Ever since you brought Ian O'Connell over here, my street cred has gone up like a million percent. I have like three hot guys in here every day."

"I'm sure you had that many over there before all that," I said.

"Maybe," she said. "But not as much. For real, Gabby, that was one of the raddest things I've ever been a part of. He was just so cool. And gorgeous."

"Agreed."

"So is he like . . ."

"Just friends," I said. "I've known him since high school."

"I definitely saw a spark," Lennox pressed on.

"Okay," I said sarcastically, while inside wondering what she was picking up on.

"Anyway," she said, sensing my stonewall, "I was just checking out The Pine Needlers' Facebook Page again, and you guys are killing it. Killing it with kindness as they say."

She was right.

Cle Elum, Roslyn, and the surrounding areas *were* killing it.

We had dozens of new GLAs added to the FB page every day. From our small community to people's relatives all across the country who joined the cause to people who just happened upon it.

The B&B's huge back room was now Kindness Quilt Central. And my apartment living room, much to the annoyance of Iris, who proposed I pay more in rent "because of all the freaking yarn" was Kindness Cap Central.

The whole thing was catching on like crazy, including my own little goals and caps. I was still doing temp jobs. I was still pouring water into my shampoo bottle. I was still was diving face first into the crazy dating experiment. But I felt a whole heck of a lot better as I did all those things. And all because a girl named Lennox decided to take what life gave her and turn it into something good.

"Well you're one inspiring young lady, Lennox!" I paused and raised my voice about an octave. "Thank you! I'm sure I'm not a hundred and ten percent better than the Long Island Medium! Okay, if you insist!"

"Whatthe heck?" Lennox said.

"My boss was walking by," I whispered into the phone.

"Oh," she said. "I see. Though, hate to break it to you, you are no Theresa Caputo."

"Obviously!"

"Well listen," Lennox said, "the in-betweens are throwing our own little Halloween party, since Monday we did the whole Trick-or-Treat in the hospital thing, and getting together on Saturday was basically the most fun a lot of us have hand in a long time."

"Well that makes me happy," I said.

"Yeah," Lennox continued. "So I have a question."

"I might have an answer," I said.

"And you call yourself a psychic," Lennox quipped.

"Hey," I said back. "When you find yourself at Taco Bell and you see a girl with a half-eaten Chessy Gordita Crunch heading for the trash and you think for a split second about asking her if you can have it, then we'll talk."

"Whoa," Lennox said.

"Yeah."

"So . . . anyway . . ." Lennox continued. "Did you see my post about Halloween costumes?"

I sure did.

"Well it looks like I'm going as a flapper. But no way am I going to ask the 'rents for some costume money. So . . . do you happen to have any cool friends who—"

"This is your lucky day!" I said. "Paige was a flapper this year."

Paige is obsessed with Halloween. She throws a big party every year. This year, she'd given our apartment this creepy, cool vibe with black and gold pumpkins, candles everywhere, and super creative treats she spent all weekend making.

"Nurse Paige?"

"The one and only."

"No way!"

"Talk about a lucky break," I said.

"What were you this year?" Lennox asked.

"I was a cat," I said. "I'm always a cat."

"Why?"

"Because . . . swear you won't laugh?"

"Sure"

"Fine. When I saw a senior in high school, I liked this boy named, let's call him, Gil."

"Gil?" Lennox said, none to impressed with the name.

"Anyway," I said. "*Gil* invited me to his Halloween party, and I was thrilled. So, I did what I always do: I researched. I found out that he hated sports, played the guitar, and ate a vegan diet. So I, being me, showed up to a high school Halloween party dressed as a can of pinto beans holding some drumsticks."

"Oh my gosh!"

"It gets worse," I said. "Because when people asked what I was, mostly because I kept accidentally knocking people over all night, I told them I was 'cool beans.'"

"I can't believe I know you," Lennox said. "And, it's decided, I'm going as a flapper."

"Good choice."

"Well thanks for the help, Gabby," Lennox said. "With, you know, a lot of stuff."

"Right back at you kid," I said. "Have a great Halloween party!"

Dear Dater,
Here is the info for Fourth Friday date:

Who: Ryan Blanding
What: Bowling
Where: Spin Alley
When: Friday 7–9 p.m.
Twists: 2

Here's the thing. When you're penniless, and you just got a job rejection email from Build-A-Bear, you realize it's time to seize the moment.

That's what I decided to do with Ryan Blanding: seize the moment. All the books say to "always be networking." So. Here I went.

After getting our shoes and setting up our lane, we got into a groove of bowling and chatting.

"So what do you do, Gabby?" asked Ryan, who, if his greying temples were an indicator, was probably about ten years older than me.

"I'm a teacher," I said, standing up straight, ball in my hand. I was dressed in my best business suit. I looked a little out of place in the bowling alley. So I put on athletic wristbands I found in the bathroom to try and casual myself up. I swung back and let it roll.

"Nice shot!"

Ryan was praising the three bowling pins I'd managed to knock over, which was actually pretty sweet.

"I appreciate that," I said as I walked toward our little cove of seats. "I find that being encouraging is better than focusing on the negative. It's something I really try to implement in my teaching. 'Good effort' is so much more helpful than 'That was terrible, kid.'"

"Mmm hmm." Ryan took his shots and got a strike.

"A strike," I said with a nod. "Not unlike the Great Southwest Railroad Strike of 1866."

I put my fingers over the fan and picked up my ball. "Isn't it interesting. This bowling ball. It's round. Like a head. A head full of ideas ready to be spun down the alley of life. And right now, I'm in charge of this ball. It's in my hands. And I will work with all my might to make sure that it doesn't end up in the gutter. That it knows what Pi is. That is understands where Penicillin comes from. That it is fascinated by the stars, intrigued by the—

Then the kid waiting in the lane next to me said, "Hey, lady, are you going to bowl or not?"

"Yes, youth of today! I am going to! But remember," I said, looking at the group of teens intensely. "The mediocre teacher tells. The good teacher explains. The superior teacher demonstrates. The great teacher inspires."

And then . . . I proceeded to throw it right into the gutter.

About half an hour later, we were in the snackbar, eating nachos and sodas when the second "twist" came in.

I thought Ryan getting to pick the place and activity was both twists. But apparently I was wrong.

Twist #2: Do the Bucket List Challenge: Name three things on your bucket list. Have your date do the same.

A bucket list challenge. I don't have a bucket list. If I did it would probably be more accurate to call it, *Yeah Right Gabby Don't You Wish list!*

And then it hit me. He wouldn't care about how lame my life goals were if he were being dazzled by my teacherly ways. Which I just read an article about . Three top qualities in great teachers: Education, organization, communication.

So I went first.

"Well." I took a sip of my drink. "I—a woman with a Bachelor's degree in secondary education from UC Berkeley—have a bottle of shower gel that I was not fully satisfied with, and I plan to return it."

"That's . . . a good one," Ryan said.

"How about you?" I asked.

"I want to learn how to play golf."

"Respectable," I said. "Well, for me, given that I am super organized, I've always kind of wanted to try almond milk."

"Cool." Ryan nodded. "I've always secretly wanted to get my pilot's license."

"That is so awesome!" I said. "All that inertia and—" Wait. What else? Planes always threw me off a little bit. "Landing gear."

"I think it's more about the idea of freedom," Ryan said with a shrug.

"Totally," I said as I held a chip in the air just shy of my mouth. "Just like it says in the Declaration of Independence: Let freedom ring. Let the white dove sing. Let the whole world know that today is a day of reckoning." Oh. Wait. I'm mixing up the Declaration of Independence with that Martina McBride song "Independence Day." "Well. You know the rest."

"Where did you say you work again?" Ryan asked.

"I didn't say." I wiped at my mouth with a napkin. "Dalton Academy."

"Oh wow." He looked completely shocked that a girl who mixed an unspeakably important document with a country-pop song worked at such a place.

"But I'm actually looking for something new," I said. "I just really want to communicate. Communicate, like, real good and stuff."

"Really?" I could see the cogs working in Ryan's mind. "Because I think I told you this on our speed date, but I'm opening this tutoring center, and I'm still not fully staffed. So maybe you'd consider applying."

"Actually," I admitted. "I think I already may have."

"Oh." Ryan looked almost deflated. "So is that why you chose me to go out?"

"Nope." I gave him a genuine smile. "We were put together randomly."

We finished eating and bucket listing and Ryan walked me out to my car. He promised to look for my resume and I told him I'd look into good deals on golf lessons.

Then after a quick hug good bye, I filled out my post-date survey under the bright lights in the parking lot.

Q: Rate the Fun of this date on this scale: Riding the subway, riding a bike, riding a rollercoaster

A: Riding a bike. (And a really nice bike, at that.)

Chapter Sixteen

"Hey guys!" I called into the open door of the B&B. "I have tons of hats for us to attach books to."

Lizette's friend Riley was donating her time and talents to make our "kindness stories" with the help of the graphic design company she owned.

"He didn't leave!" Annie came out of nowhere and grabbed onto my wrists.

"What?" I looked into her eyes, which were all wild. "Who didn't leave?"

"He's still here!" Annie repeated, squeezing my wrists a bit. "There have been sightings."

"What do you mean sightings?"

Suddenly Kit and Lizette appeared in the front room. "You told her, didn't you?" Lizette said to Annie.

"I saw her first."

"That's the same thing you said about Tyson R."

"I can't believe you're bringing up Tyson R. right now!"

"Ladies." Kit set down a box that appeared to be full of fabric. "How about we all tell her."

"Yes, how about that," I said.

"Ian's back," they said in unison.

"He is?" My voice was high. I cleared my throat and lowered my voice a couple octaves. "I mean he is?"

"Yes!" Lizette said. "I mean, we think."

"You think."

The Pine Needlers went on to describe the mysterious sightings that led them to believe Ian was back. Every night at 11 p.m., someone wearing all black rode a skateboard down First Street. There were mysterious footprints on the baseball field. The lights were sometimes on at night at the Irish Rose.

Then somehow, I really don't know how, we all ended up dressed in black head to toe, with black Kindness Caps on our heads, hiding in the shrubs behind the Irish Rose Inn.

"He's in there!" Annie was on Lizette's shoulders, looking in the window I used to stalk Ian from. It was all boarded up, since it was only being used as a vacation home now, so the only place to see in was the very top.

"Seriously?" I said.

"I think so," she answered. "I mean, I can only see his back, but it looks like Ian's back."

"Well, get him to turn around," Lizette said.

"How is she supposed to do that?" Kit, our lookout, asked.

Annie tapped the glass.

"Annie!" I whisper-yelled.

"I'm just trying to see his face . . . oh my gosh!" She gasped. "I think he saw me."

"Run!" I said.

Annie jumped down faster than I've ever seen her do anything and we all ran to her SUV, laughing so hard our stomachs hurt as she "peeled out" onto the street at a very fast 35 MPH.

I love my Pine Needlers.

Everyone in the world should be lucky enough to have some Pine Needlers in their life.

"So it was definitely him?" I asked when we were on the road that led back to the B&B.

"One hundred percent sure," Annie said.

"I wonder what happened," I said.

And luckily for me, I didn't have to wait too long to find out.

At exactly 11:11 p.m., as I sat in my little attic room knitting while watching Netflix, it happened.

Something straight out of the young adult novels I know I'm too old to read, but don't care.

Ian texted me, *I see that your light is on. I'm out front. Can you come down?*

I slipped on my thickest sweater and Converse and practically ran down the stairs.

"Hey." Ian was leaning against his truck.

"Hey." I walked toward him. "So you're back?"

"More like I never got on the plane," he said.

"So you've been hanging out here for the past week?"

"Trying to lay low," he said. "I parked my truck and I've just been using my old skateboard to get around. And I've gone out to the ball field a few times."

"Wow." I rubbed my hands together. "I totally did not know any of that information whatsoever."

Ian nodded, blowing warm air onto his cold hands.

"Come in for some cocoa," I said.

"Like old times," Ian said.

"Yep."

We padded into the quiet, empty kitchen and I made us both big mugs of cocoa, his manly and straight up, mine girly and complete with whipped cream and sprinkles.

"Can I ask you something?" I said, taking a seat on a bar stool.

"You," Ian said, "can ask me anything."

"Is Lauren . . . did she decide to come back after all?"

"Nope." Ian sat down next to me. "She's still in Denver."

"And you guys are?"

"We are the reason 'It's Complicated' is a legitimate relationship status."

"Ah." I nodded as I took a sip of cocoa and got whipped cream on my nose.

Ian reached out and wiped it off. "Do you remember when I won the pie-eating contest at the fair?" he asked.

"Of course I remember." We'd spent the whole week walking around that fair. Ian had won me a bright pink elephant, which I still have in my closet, in the bottle knocking game. He was the only person I ever saw win. And I cheered him on as he entered the pie eating contest. And in between those moments we talked. I talked about the crazy towns I'd lived in over the years and how I had an irrational fear of flies. He swore he'd take me to

Portillo's, his favorite hot dog place in Chicago, someday. And told me he secretly wanted to get married in Ireland.

"And afterward you brought me here and nursed me back to health," Ian said, his voice breaking into my memories.

"That's right. I totally forgot about that. I made you lay on the couch and I turned on *One Tree Hill* and you said it was making you sicker."

Ian laughed softly. Then he looked around the still, quiet B&B. "What is it about this place? About you?"

"What do you mean?"

"I mean, I could throw a baseball anywhere in this place and I'd have a memory there of you, like trying to do the *New York Times* crossword together without any outside help at that dining room table."

"That's right." I peered at the table. "It took us like a month."

"Standing at the stove, making Fruity Pebbles treats."

"They're so underrated," I said.

"You even got pretty good at catch out there." Ian pointed to the backyard.

"And you got good at finding new bands that I liked."

"It was easy," Ian said. "I just listened for anything with slow guitar and a depressed-sounding singer."

"Hey!" I playfully smacked his arm. Then I moved my mug up to my mouth and took in a breath, steam rising to my lips. "You were one heck of a friend."

"And what am I now?" he asked softly.

What was he? He was the best part of my favorite memories. He was the guy who didn't think for a second about driving hours to give a little light to some sick kids.

He was the guy who I could see in every chapter of the rest of my life. He was the guy who hadn't gone to Denver.

Problem was, he was also a guy with a girl who was obviously dying to make things right with him.

I was sure of that because I knew what it was like to have Ian O'Connell in your life.

"Ian." I blinked and felt this aching inside that I only *thought* was bad when I was a teenager.

"Gabby." His eyes were pleading. "I need you to give me something here."

"I can—"

Creak.

We both started at the sound.

"Oh. I'm sorry, kids." Kit, wearing a robe over her pajamas, pulled an apologetic face.

"It's okay," I said, turning my head away to wipe away the tears. "I think Ian was just about ready to leave."

Chapter Seventeen

Dear Dater,
    You have just one date left. And before we choose the details, we need a little information.
    Please meet us in Room 410 of the sociology building at Pacific Credence University tonight at 7 p.m.
    See you then!

I got the message this morning.

And now here I am, alone in room 410, wondering if I'm in the wrong place.

I was about to get up to try and figure out what was going on when research assistant Jen walked into the room.

"Hi, Gabby!"

"Hi."

"Can you fill this out for me?" She handed me a paper survey.

"Sure."

"Dr. Whitmore will be in soon."

"Oh. Cool. I'll finally get to meet her."

Jen didn't say anything. Just raised her eyebrows before retreating from the room.

All right. What do we have here?

I read the letters on the top: *Five Fridays Study Survey*

Please answer the following questions honestly and completely.

How would you rate the amount of fun you had on each of your dates on this scale: Watching Paint Dry. Playing Twister with Your Parents. Watching Okay TV. Watching a 3D Movie. Riding a Roller Coaster.

Date #2 Roarke: Watching a 3D movie. (Mostly because he did me a major solid.)

Date #3 Paul: Watching Okay TV. (Though I did spend much of it thinking I was going to die.)

Date #4 Ryan: Watching a 3D Movie.

Date #5 Dillon: Watching paint dry.

Please rate the romantic chemistry you felt with your dates using this scale: I have a bigger crush on Elmo. I could see us being friends. I might kiss him on a special occasion. I can really see this one going somewhere. I haven't ever felt anything like this before.

Date #2 Roarke: I might kiss him on a special occasion.

Date #3 Paul: I might kiss him on a special occasion.

Date #4 Ryan: I could see us being friends.

Date #5 Dillon: Right now, I can honestly say, it's somewhere between friends and Elmo.

Would you like to date any of these men again? Use one of the following answers: I am never, ever, ever; not at all; that might be kind of cool; sure, sounds good! I'm ready right now!

Date #2 Roarke: That might be kind of cool.
Date #3 Paul: That might be kind of cool.
Date #4 Ryan: Not at all (sorry Ryan).
Date #5 Dillon: Hmm . . .

How have your "Saturdates" been? Well. You asked for totally honesty. So here goes. Normally I'd probably be writing about how I spend my Saturday nights doing laundry, hoping a cute guy will ask me if I have any quarters. But something crazy happened. And instead I've spent the past few Saturdays with the boy I fell in love with at sixteen. And I'm pretty sure I've fallen in love with him all over again.

"I'm done!" I sat alone for a minute then opened the door, looking into the dark hall for any signs of life.

But I didn't see anyone.

I don't watch many slasher movies.

But I do know that this is pretty much how they all start.

Girl sits alone somewhere dark and mysterious wearing something provocative.

Or in my case: in a pair of dress pants that she colors in with marker to disguise the bleach stains.

Then girl sees scary entity.

Or in my case: Dr. Brooke Whitmore. Sister of Lauren. Author of study.

"This is a crazy coincidence," I said in shock, my hand clutching the survey because I had just written that I was falling in love with her sister's "It's Complicated" guy.

"Could be." She was drinking a red drink that looked EXACTLY like blood. I think it was the viscosity. "Or it could be that you, Dater 410, were perfect for the study."

"Wait." I frowned. "What do you mean?"

"There's someone outside waiting for you," she said.

I know it's crazy. But as I shot up and moved for the door, I almost expected to see Ian standing there.

I told you it was crazy.

Because obviously it wasn't Ian.

It was . . .

"Hi, Gab."

Dillon.

I'm not going to lie, my heart still quickened a tiny bit at the sight of him. Which kind of confused the heck out of me.

"What are you doing here?" I asked.

"What I've been waiting to do since I answered an email asking me to join a dating study with you."

"You got that?"

Dillon nodded. "Last week."

Last week? I thought. But they'd gone out a long time ago. He must have meant he just opened it last week. Typical Dillon.

"I'll let you two get to it," Lauren's big sister said. "Keep that survey. It's the end of the study survey, so now you're all done. Bye!"

"Bye." We both waved, and I just stood there for a moment to get my bearings.

"So . . . what about your girl . . . the . . . ?"

"There was never anything there with Daisy." Dillon shoved his hands in his pockets. "She was just an excuse for my issues. And we can talk about all that stuff later. But first. Here." Dillon handed me an envelope.

Photo Scavenger Hunt: Photo #1.

"You always said you wanted to do one," Dillon said.

I looked into his eyes. "Yeah, I did. But that was before—"

"Gabby." Dillon took my hand into his. "I did everything wrong. And I plan to spend many, many hours telling you all about what an idiot I know I am and figuring out what we're supposed to be. But for tonight I was thinking maybe you could just let me do something for you that I should have done a long, long time ago."

I stared at him, my look softening.

"Consider this envelope #1 of me trying to make things right," he said.

"Go ahead." He nodded toward the envelope. "Open it."

I carefully slid my finger under the flap and read the card inside. "Get a photo of yourself in the kids' area of a fast food restaurant."

Dillon raised his eyebrows.

"You're going to do this?" I asked.

Dillon nodded.

"All right," I said, a hint of disbelief in my voice.

"She said yes!" Dillon whooped. Loudly. And Dillon is so not a whooper. Then he carried me piggyback out to his car, which was just beside mine in the parking lot.

And that started my first photo scavenger hunt.

#1: In the kids area of a fast food restaurant.

We slid down the slide in a McDonald's PlayPlace and got a dirty look from a woman whose kids were waiting to go down while we snapped the photo.

#2: Doing a cartwheel.

Turns out Dillon can do a cartwheel. I can not.

#3: Pointing to an out-of-state license plate.

I found a Nebraska one. Dillon found Alaska.

#4: Walking a dog.

After trying three times and having one guy snap my photo and say, "I'm reporting you," we finally found a really cool couple with a Great Dane. Now that was a picture.

Around Photo #5—Playing a video game in a store—I started to relax. I was actually having fun with Dillon.

In a way it almost felt like old times but better as we got photos of the following:

#6: A stranger holding a piece of paper where Dillon— so not the type of guy to do that kind of thing—wrote Gabby + Dillon and drew a heart around it.

#7: Sitting on a bench. (That one was a selfie of us both.)

#8: Doing whatever a sign says. I took a photo of Dillon "stopping." It was cool to see a looser, goofier side of him.

#9: On a merry-go-round. We found a little park and spun until we were dizzy.

I loved it.

Then, as the adrenaline began to slow I said, "Thanks for this Dillon. It's kind of nice just . . . being normal with you."

"It is nice." Dillon stood up and gently pulled on one of the metal bars, sending me in a slow circle. "And Gabby?"

"Yeah."

"I really am sorry."

"I know."

"And I really do want to figure out what this is supposed to be. Once and for all."

I stared at Dillon. This handsome, brilliant, charming doctor who I had wished upon wishes would come back to me. But all I could think of was Ian. Looking at me like he had in the B&B kitchen.

"So what made you change your mind?" I asked Dillon.

Dillon shook his head. "It started to change it when I saw you with that guy Blaze."

"About that," I said, "You were there as part of the study, weren't you?"

"No." He shook his head. "I didn't even know there *was* a study."

"Seriously?" I narrowed my eyes, convinced it couldn't be true. "So you just happened to end up at the Crab Pot?"

"Yeah." Dillon scratched his head. "I think I got an email from them about a special. Or a text about a coupon. Something.Anyway, seeing you with someone else was tough."

"Yeah, well, I saw Daisy kiss you that same night."

"That was a mistake." Dillon stared at the moving merry-go-round. "I was thinking of the cheerleader who never gave me the time of day in high school." Dillon shook his head. "I don't know what I was thinking."

"And then I saw you with Ian O'Connell," Dillon said. "And that was kind of it for me."

"So you're telling me, when you saw me with other guys, that's when you decided you want to really give us a chance."

"I have a problem with it, I think," Dillon said. "You know, commitment."

"I've always thought people will only have a problem with commitment until they find the right person for them."

"Maybe that's why I'm here with you right now."

"Maybe." I watched as he ran for a minute then jumped.

I held on tight until the spinning stopped.

And then I had an idea.

"So, there are twists on these study dates," I said to Dillon.

"What kind of twists?"

"Well," I said. "The twist right now is that we have to play Two Truths and One Lie."

Dillon scrunched his face up in what I'd describe as his untrusting doctor face. You know that saying about how doctors are taught that their patients are always lying to them. That kind of face. "And how do you know that's our twist?"

"Because the app said so." I held up my phone.

"Oh." Dillon nodded. "Let's do it, then."

"Awesome. Here are my three. You ready?"

"I'm ready."

"My favorite cereal is Cocoa Puffs. My favorite type of food is Italian. And every time my dad sees me he makes me play something for him on the guitar."

"Trick question," Dillon said instantly. "All three are true."

"Hmm." I breathed in deeply and rested my back on the not-very-comfortable merry-go-round bar. "I'm afraid you're wrong."

"No I'm not." Dillon narrowed his eyes.

"Cocoa Puffs are not my favorite cereal. In fact, I think they taste a little metallic."

"What?" Dillon looked so confused. "So why do you always buy them then?"

I lay on my back and looked up at the stars. "Because the end result is worth it."

Dillon didn't say anything.

"Do you want to know something crazy?" I said, still lying down.

I could feel him tense. "Do I?"

I sat up and gripped the nearest bar. "If we would have done this a couple of months ago, heck even a couple weeks ago, I would likely have told you that I knew what this was supposed to be."

"But?" Dillon searched my face. "What's changed?"

"Everything."

Chapter Eighteen

I never drove so recklessly in my life.

I didn't even stop off at home first. I just hopped in the car and drove—blasting the Gabby & Ian Summer '06 CD mix Ian had for made me in—feeling clarity like I'd never felt before.

When I got to the Irish Rose, I was so pumped with adrenaline that I didn't notice the extra cars in the driveway, I didn't care that I couldn't remember if I brushed my teeth that morning, I just banged on the door. "Ian!" I yelled. "Ian!"

And that's when the door swung open.

And I was face to face with . . .

Lauren.

"Oh. Hi, Lauren." I tried to think with my mind as my heart split in two. "I just came over to remind everyone that the supermarket has two-for-one canned green beans."

I have no idea what her reaction was.

Because I was already in my car, hot tears of anger/ humiliation/regret and everything in between rolling down my cheeks.

"Gabby." Kit looked up from her sewing machine and stopped what she was doing. "What happened?"

"I . . ." Tears streamed down my cheeks. "I love him." I wiped at my face. "But I think he loves her."

"Oh sweetie. Come sit down." Kit took me by the elbow and led me out of the master and to the back room.

Annie, Lizette, and about four other quilters I recognized from town were hard at work binding, ironing, and perfecting the Kindness Quilts. They all waved to me without looking up.

They were women on a mission.

I waved back and was about to sit next to Lizette— who was perched on the couch, doing some detail work— when something happened to me.

"Oh my gosh," I said. Slowly I walked over to a stack of six quilts. I took the small, brown paper bag material booklet that was attached to it with twine and a tiny safety pin in my hand. It was so perfectly done.

I flipped through the booklet's pages.

Dear Recipient,

This is no ordinary quilt. It is a Kindness Quilt. Each block represents a good deed done. This book contains the story of the twelve good deeds, the kindness, sewn into the stitches of your new quilt. Use it well!

Gave someone else the good parking spot

Hid a few dollars around the dollar store
Cut my neighbor's lawn
Left a tub of detergent at the Laundromat
Left a Post-It on my neighbor's mailbox
Played the piano at a retirement home
Sang old songs with my grandparents
Donated books to the women's shelter
Bought way too many Girl Scout cookies
Taught my grandma how to use Twitter
Dropped change into an expired parking meter

And then, there it was.

Bought donuts for a family wearing family reunion t-shirts

It was mine.

Mine and Ian's.

Suddenly it was like the fog lifted from my brain and I saw everything clearly for the first time.

All along I'd been looking for the wrong thing.

Someone who made me feel lucky.

But I, a woman of faith, believed in something much bigger than luck. I believed in blessings.

Dillon made me feel lucky. Lucky I found a cute doctor. Lucky he liked me back.

Ian made me feel something different altogether. He made me feel blessed. Blessed to know him. Blessed to have shared memories with him.

And the thing is, when you realize you're blessed, that there's a power much bigger than luck at play, you find yourself wanting to share that feeling. That's why I had homemade CDs from Ian and store-bought trinkets from Dillon. That's why Ian jumped at the chance to go to the hospital when he didn't have to and Dillon seemed to be fairly satisfied with what he was already doing.

And that's when I knew exactly what I had to do.

Ian, I texted with shaky fingers as I stood right in the middle of the busy room, I need to talk to you.

And then, after an agonizing two minutes of those darn three little "someone is texting you" dots, he responded, I'll come by tomorrow.

The same words he said to me ten years ago.

Chapter Nineteen

I thought there were going to be snacks." Lizette looked around the classroom with a confused expression.

"What do you mean snacks?" I asked.

"Like popcorn and candy," Lizette said

"What?"

"That's half the reason you come to a play."

"We're not at a play," I said. "We're at the We're at the conclusion seminar for the Five Fridays dating study, where we get to learn what it was all about." We'd been told we could bring family, so I'd brought Lizette and Paige. Kit and Annie offered to stay back at the B&B to get ready for the quilt auction. I had no idea where Iris was.

"I thought we were here to watch *His Girl Friday*."

"No matter," she pulled something out of her purse. "Some cute college boy offered me this brownie."

"No!" Lizette and I shouted as I grabbed it.

"What?"

"Hello and welcome!" Dr. Chan spoke into the microphone. "We'll keep this brief since we know it's getting close to the holidays and you all have lots to do. Jen."

Jen stood up. I looked around the room and saw that a few of the girls in the room were holding hands with guys. Interesting. "Hi daters and guests! Thank you for coming to our post-study seminar. Daters, if you will take a moment to look, you should find a single question on your apps. Please answer that question."

I clicked and read.

Were you successful over the course of this study in finding a relationship?

No, I typed.

Then my mind shot back to the text I'd sent the night before.

The text I hadn't heard a single thing about since.

Jen went on for a while about the idea behind the study, the making of the app, and other stuff that I kind of tuned out because I knew it would all be in the abstract.

But then, a PowerPoint slide of an overview of the experiment showed up in front of the room as a hard copy of it was being passed down the aisles.

The Dating Experiment: The Method Behind Our Madness

Purpose/Question: Are romantic partners chosen better when algorithms are used or when human autonomy is used to make choices?

Research: Every dating site and app ever.

Hypothesis: Given a five-week dating period, we believe our algorithm will lead to more relationships.

Experiment: Everything we've been doing for the past five weeks.

Analysis: Everything we've been doing for the past five weeks.

Conclusion: People fared better when they chose for themselves, but we believe this is just due to the time period. Be prepared for our next project, Ten Tuesdays!

A girl's hand shot up. She didn't wait to be called on before speaking. "Why did the study invite everyone in my social media network, when I asked for it to only invite a few."

"Yeah! It did that to me too."

"Me too!"

Murmurs filled the room.

"You will all receive a comprehensive write up of this study," Jen said. "Until then, some details will be a little hazy."

Wait a minute.

I scrutinized the paper in my hands.

This wasn't hazy at all.

The women were right. I bet there wasn't a single woman who had sent invites to everyone. The study had.

Of course.

It all made sense now.

I knew I hadn't invited my butcher, my baker, and my candlestick maker. (Okay, I don't actually have any one of those, but it seemed fitting.)

They weren't following any rules at all. Which meant from the very beginning Brooke/Brooklyn (suddenly the Carl/Carlyle thing made more sense) had seen it all. Everything I thought about love. Everything I thought about Ian. Everything I thought when I was with Ian. And I wasn't an idiot. I was protected by some privacy, but all she had to do was call her sister a "research assistant," and the two of them could sit around and talk about all my deepest Ian secrets.

"If you have any more questions," Jen said. "We're lucky to have our lead researcher Brooke Whitmore with us."

And that's when Lauren's sister stepped out.

"I want to thank you all for participating in this study!"

"Oh my gosh," Lizette said. "Did you know she was—"

"Yes," I said snappily.

"Do you want to—" Paige began.

"No."

No. Freaking. NO!

I shot up out of my seat and ignored the death stares and exaggerated "ouch"es as I got out of the row. I threw the door open, climbed the stairs to the backstage area and waited.

I think if I was a little bit crazier—which unfortunately for you I'm not because it would make one heck of a scene—I think I would have pushed my way onto the stage and confronted the good doctor there.

"Thank you again!" I heard her saying from my spot in the wings. "You have helped us make the best product we can! And don't forget to watch for our next project as Dr. Chan mentioned!"

The crowd was still clapping when suddenly I felt a familiar sensation: a cold hand touching my arm.

"Hi, Gabby."

"What did you do?" I asked her.

"Nothing that wasn't permitted." She tugged on the cuffs of her shirt. "I didn't jeopardize the research."

"This whole study has been so . . . off, and I couldn't put my finger on it, but now I realize that you guys were doing whatever you wanted to do."

"And?"

"And I need you to tell me what you did with me."

"The same as everyone else."

"But there was more with me," I said. "I know there was."

"It's really not that scandalous," Brooke said. "Mostly your dates were just like everyone else's. But there were times when I had to make sure you went on the dates that were best."

Suddenly, my own extremities felt cold. Because she meant the dates that were best for *Lauren*. Not for me. For her sister.

Suddenly, it all came to my mind, like flashes on a movie screen. I spoke as if reading subtitles.

"Lauren was confused and off to see Carlyle. I went out with my old friend and a 'twist' told me to make it romantic. Good for Lauren.

"Then when Lauren changed her mind, but Ian wasn't rushing back fast enough, you read the stuff I wrote and decided to put me on a date with my recent ex. Good for Lauren."

"Except it's not," Brooke said. "I might have let it slip to Ian that you and Dillon have reconciled."

"What?" I shook my head. "He'll never believe that."

"Oh but a picture speaks a thousand words," Brooke said.

And that's when it came crashing into my mind like a cold ocean wave. "The scavenger hunt," I said, my breath shallow.

"They're cute pictures," Brooke said.

I felt tears well in my eyes. "Why did you do this?"

"I'm the only one here to take care of Lauren," she said. "My father is gone. And he took most of my mother with him." A hint of deep sadness crossed her face. "Someone has to look out for this family."

"I'm going to choose to believe you did what you did out of some kind of love," I said, wiping my face with the back of my hand. "But what if Lauren and Ian aren't meant to be together? What if there is a greater love out there for her?"

"Then I'll make sure she finds him."

"Good to hear," I said. "Get ready to start looking."

Because Ian was my great love. And he was going to show up at the B&B this time.

I knew it.

Chapter Twenty

I stepped into the B&B, all chilly and hurting from the morning, and was delighted to find the whole place decked out in subtle, beautiful holiday decorations. White lights and candles were everywhere, and accents of silver cheered everything up. The cozy, casual feel of the place was perfect. The fireplace was roaring, the apple cider was, whatever cider does. Wassailing?

And the place was full of people.

I thought this was going to be a bit of an intimate thing.

But the place was abuzz.

The press was there.

And by press I mean both Lizette with a Press Pass and also a guy who came out from Seattle.

There were blown-up photos of some of Ian's celebrity friends wearing Kindness Caps. (I had no idea he did that.) And posters of the eight gorgeous Kindness Quilts.

I was suddenly overwhelmed by just how many people had put their hearts and souls into this thing.

I stopped in my tracks next to the display of Kindness Caps on the dining room table. They'd been arranged in the most beautiful way. My insides warmed as I looked at them. And there, in the middle of the hats, was a cool photo collage of me trying to teach Ian how to knit. I remembered that like it was yesterday.

The whole B&B was bustling with people getting food, admiring the quilts, and reading some of the GLAs that were framed and placed in all the common areas. I made my way into the den to get an up-close look at the quilts. They were stunning. Each and every one had its own story. As I stood and admired the works of art, it dawned on me that I'd really been in two studies these past couple months. One taught me who I'm in love with. The other taught me the what love really is.

I went into the kitchen where Kit put her arm around me.

"This is awesome," I said.

"Don't you love when an idea turns into . . . something?"

I nodded and tilted my head into her shoulder.

"Go bid on some of the quilts," Kit said.

"I wish," I said. "I'm finally in the black, but no way can I win one of the quilts."

"Did I say anything about winning?" Kit said, a telling twinkle in her eye.

"All right then." I started making my way to the den, where all the quilts were being displayed/auctioned.

"Tell me who this would look better on." Lizette, followed closely by Annie, held a cute blue knit cap with a pink heart on it. "Me or Annie?"

"Those hats are for the kids!" I grabbed it from her hand. "But, since you're thinking of your sister, tell you what, I'll make you both one."

"You want to know something I was thinking about?" Annie asked me.

"Sure."

"These past couple months, you've been talking about how you've failed to get a teaching job. But look around. You may not have been paid for it, but you taught us about this. You were our teacher." Annie kissed my cheek and waved at a friend in the distance. "Remember that."

I felt warm and wonderful as I continued on into the front room/den and admired the first quilt in the semi-circle display, looking down at its bid sheet as I did.

There were a few bids.

But there at the bottom of the sheet was this: *highest bid plus $1,000. Quilt to go to the second highest bidder.*

Interesting.

I moved to the next quilt.

Same thing.

And the next.

And the next.

Every single bid sheet had the same thing written on it.

My soul sang. Because I knew exactly who made those bids, though his writing was a lot neater than I remembered it.

It was the guy who came back to Cle Elum every winter to look after the Irish Rose. The guy who started a free summer baseball camp for kids who can't afford things like summer baseball camps. The guy who buys boxes upon boxes of Girl Scout cookies even though his training does not allow him to eat them. (Though I swear I've seen him sneak a few.) The guy who taught me everything I know about Good Little Anythings.

The guy who was now a man, the man I loved with every atom in my body, was here.

I stood on my tiptoes and searched the crowd.

I knew he'd be here.

"So tell me." It was Lizette speaking into a voice recorder, trying to sound all official. "What brings you to today's event?"

"He's here," I said. "Ian's here."

She turned off the recorder. "Are you serious?"

"Thank you all for coming out!" Kit's voice boomed on the B&B's event microphone. "The silent auction is now closed, and we are pleased to announce that thanks to an anonymous donor we have over $40,000 to donate to Project Good Little Anything and Seattle Pediatric Hospital. And an upcoming delivery of 340 Kindness Caps!"

Everyone cheered.

"And now," Kit continued, "we have a special guest, whose arm I twisted until they agreed to say something."

Ian?

My whole body was on high alert.

But instead of Ian, I saw Lennox appear on the big TV on the main wall of the room. "Hey everyone!" She waved from her hospital bed, a ton of friends and family gathered around her.

Everyone in the B&B cheered.

"Since Kit insisted that I show you all my mug, I thought it was the least I could do to thank you for all you've done for me, for us. So I wrote a few things down that I wanted to say. A little bit of how I feel."

Everyone in the room got quiet. Aunt Kit came up beside me and held my hand. And as tears filled my eyes, I looked across the room and saw Ian, his emotions all over his face.

Our eyes met and we exchanged smiles that may have looked small to anyone looking on. But not to us.

"This money is going to do a lot of good," Lennox said. "So I thank you from the bottom of my heart. But I want you all to know that equally as important are the good things that went into it. Last night I stayed up reading an email that Annie Thompson sent me. An email that listed every single Good Little Anything that has gone into your caps and your quilts. Everything from 'I told my brother he did good at his soccer game' to 'I held my friend's hand during chemo.' Recently, a friend of mine got me thinking about luck. And here's the thing I realized: it's basically totally bogus. Crooks get rich. Kids get sick. But there is a very, very big difference between being lucky and being blessed. There's not much you can do about luck. I mean, maybe you can wear the same underwear for an entire football season—yes, Joe Fisher, I know all about it—"

Laughter sounded in the room as people brushed away tears.

And that's when I saw my mom and dad walk in. They saw me and waved.

"You can put good thoughts out into the universe, get lucky with a psychic—wink wink, Gabby Malone—or make it to the top of whatever ladder you're climbing. But being blessed? That's something that you get when you give."

I looked over at Ian. He looked right back. "We reached the same conclusion," I said softly, every bit the science nerd I loved to be.

"I started this blog because we all get pounded with the life thing and the luck thing," Lennox continued. "But there is an antidote. It won't cure you. But it will change you. And it's crazy, somehow, the less I have to give, the more I get out of the little things I can give. I don't know how this all works. All I know is it's a miracle. Thank you all for reminding us to believe in miracles! Project Good Little Anything forever! Thanks from all of us!" She panned the camera on her phone through the room. Then she waved and she was gone.

After a wonder-filled moment of silent clarity, a city council member held up his clear mug of cider. "To Lennox and everyone like her!"

"Here, here!" A shout rang out.

When I looked to where I had seen Ian, he was gone. Where did he . . .

I spun around a few times and saw him just as he

slipped out onto "the outdoor pavilion" and headed for the patio swing that's tucked away in the backyard.

I made my way through the crowd and slid the back door open. I pulled the sweater sleeves over my hands and sat down next to him on the well-loved swing. "Hey, Mr. Quilt Bandit."

Ian smiled. "Nice solve, Nancy Drew."

"I thought you were long gone," I said. "Off to plan your wedding in Denver."

"There isn't going to be a wedding," Ian said. "And I'm going to be in town for a while."

"I'm sorry about the first part," I said. "But I'm secretly jumping inside at the second part."

Ian reached his hand over to mine. Only this time, instead of being hesitant, he locked his fingers in mine.

My fingers, my arms, the whole of my body had never felt anything better.

"So," I said. "I know you've been told some stuff about me lately."

"Trust me," Ian said. "It didn't take me long to realize the truth behind it all."

"You know what's crazy?" I said, "If I hadn't lost my job, none of this would have happened."

"Maybe."

"Well, if I never lost my job, I never would have joined the experiment."

"That's probably true." Ian reached into his pocket and handed me a letter, folded and yellowed with age. "I have something for you."

Brow furrowed, I gently unfolded the paper.

It was dated on that day he didn't show up to say good-bye.

Ten years ago.

Dear Gabby,

I wanted to say good-bye in person. But the more I thought about it, the more I realized if I tried to say good-bye in person, I might not leave. But I have to go. I need to give my family the life they deserve. They've worked so hard. But I want you to know if you find this some day, I loved you. I was so completely crazy in love with you. Your laugh. Your eyes. The way you babble when you first meet someone. The way you let people go ahead of you in line. The way you look in summer dresses. And cutoffs and a t-shirt. The stories you tell about your crazy camper life. But mostly, your beautiful soul. I've never, ever met a more beautiful one.

Love, Ian

"Ian O'Connell." I looked down at the letter. "I'm about half a second away from being in love with you. And I just need to know . . ."

"I'm more than half a second past falling in love with you." Ian brushed a strand of hair behind my ear. "And I've been waiting ten years to do this."

And then he kissed me.

It was every single thing I thought it would be and more. Intense, then soft, then intense again. It was beautiful and dreamlike, yet I never felt more awake. I gripped the swing's metal frame to keep me grounded.

"Is this really happening?" I asked.

"I can do it again until you're sure."

The End

Acknowledgments

This book should not be real. When I sit down and think about how it came to be, I just don't know how it's possible. It is absolutely a miracle in print. And, as with most miracles, there were a LOT of people who helped make this one possible.

My family: Jacob, thank you for doing all those dishes and giving me all those pep talks. Mom and Dad, thanks for getting my late night phone calls and actually picking them up. Brian, Brett, Eli, Theresa, and Vanessa, you guys are the best family a girl could have. Miranda, your friendship is priceless to me, as are our discussions about *Friends* and *The Bachelorette*. Nancy and Jack, thank you for the quilting insights and the model of a hardworking artist. And, most especially, thank you to my nieces and nephews who have shown me such love and helped heal my heart.

The wonderful MP7th: Diane, thank you for your unwavering charity. Rebecca and Kimi, thank you for helping me get my footing in this wonderful new world. Amber, you may never know what a blessing your example has been.

The amazing team at CFI: Emma, you are just as wonderful as everyone said. Emily, Hali, and Jessica, thank you for your remarkable talent and patience. And Priscilla, thank you for a cover to fall in love with.

All the friends who read my ramblings: Thank you Lori and Marley for being the kind of readers I could only dream of. Thank you friends who ask me or write to me about my books; your words have changed my life in such profound ways. With all my heart I hope this one brings you joy.

Discussion Questions

1. Are you lucky? Prove it.

2. Gabby agrees to join a dating study. What's the craziest job you've ever had? What's the craziest thing you've ever done for love?

3. Can two people who have never, ever been more than friends become something more?

4. What do you think about Lennox's Good Little Anything campaign? Would you join in?

5. If you could see the future right now, would you want to? Anything in particular?

About the Author

If I had been able to see the future in my younger years, I would have seen: I can't get enough of indie music, my native California, or my perfect nieces and nephews; I always root for the underdog; and kiwi fruit freaks me out. Also, I get to live near Salt Lake City, Utah, which would thrill younger-me, who spent many a Christmas Day wishing for a tiny flake of snow. Oh, and I highly recommend the Sunset Café in Cle Elum, Washington! Catch me online at elodiastrain.com or on Twitter and Instagram @elodiastrain.

SCAN TO VISIT

WWW.ELODIASTRAIN.COM